MR. JONES

Book 2 of the Adelaide Henson Mystery Series

William Cain

Disclaimer

Mr. Jones is a work of fiction. Any references to real people, events, establishments or locales are intended only to give this work of fiction a sense of reality and authenticity, and all are used fictitiously. All other characters, places, dialogue and events are the product of the author's imagination.

ISBN: 9781708184353

for margaret, my mother

Chicago
    DiCaprio Crime Family
        Gennarro (Biggie) Battaglia – retiring overboss – aka Ken Jones
        Elsie Jones – wife to Ken Jones
        Vincent Battaglia – overboss
        Alberto Gangi – retiring underboss, best friend to Gennarro
        Michael Seppi – cleaner
        Benito DiCaprio – retired overboss
            Consuela DiCaprio – daughter
        John (Skip) O'Hare – underling
    Spadaro Crime Family
        Anthony Spadaro – Boss, nemesis of Gennarro
        Mitch Conti – retired Consigliore
        Helen Richter – cleaner
        Victor Spadaro – deceased brother
        Ulrich Pavlov – contract killer
Miami
    DiCaprio Crime Family
        Joseph Riggoti – underboss
        Daisy Fuendes – cleaner
Asheville
    Asheville P.D.
        Commissioner Bill Evans
        Captain Keith Leary
        Detective Adelaide (Addie) Henson
        Detective Robert Hardin – partner to Addie
    FBI
        Senior Special Agent David Juvieux
        Agent Chris Forsyth
The Thomas's
    Reggi (Virginia) Thomas
    Joseph Thomas (deceased husband to Reggi)
        Frank Thomas – son
        Frédérica Thomas (divorced wife of Frank)
            Frank Jr. (Frannie) – son
            Agatha Winslow – fiancé to Frannie
        Charlotte Bouknight – daughter

Edwin Bouknight – husband to Charlotte
Madison – daughter
Haley – daughter
Megan Thomas – daughter
Patrick – son
Connor – son

Other Players
Jericho and Irene Henson – Adelaide's parents
John Paulson – Reggi's first husband and Frank's natural father
A "friendly" woman

Author's Note

This is Book Two in a series of ten books. A series that is best read in order. Each two books are closely related, meaning Book 1 and Book 2, for example, complete that main story. A story which is part of the bigger picture of all ten books. This is the reason I publish the two close together, and make them available, as an eBook, for free on some days.

I myself am a slow reader. So, I explain this to others as 'I like to digest the material. I'm not trying to read as many books as I can, and then forget about them.' I like reading and going over what the author has written years later.

Years go by, and I can still remember characters from the Follett series Pillars of the Earth; the builders, the nurse, Jack and Claris, Aliena, even Philip. These and others live on because I took the time to read them. Ken Follett is a master storyteller, and it all plays out in his epics, and his shorter stories. I read Code to Zero in one day, it was that good.

And, I've had reviewers finish both of my Books 1 and 2 in a day and a half. One even reread the two. Go figure.

So, don't rob yourself. Read them in order, and enjoy!

PREVIOUSLY

February

The Thomases

Frank Thomas walks the streets of the Upper West Side happily. He's determined in his pursuit of Adelaide. He's not giving up—he doesn't agree with her reasoning for putting their relationship on hold, about the distance and the divorce.

Boy gets girl. Boy loses girl.

No…Boy will get girl. Boy will get girl back.

Frank's mother, Reggi Thomas, knows even senior citizens can fall in love, and *she's* fallen in love with Ken Jones. None of her children can stop her. Not Frank, not Megan, and not Charlotte.

Since meeting him in September, after Joe died, she's been seeing him more and more. She needed, wanted, him. He knew it, he wanted her too.

She would never once in a million years dream

she'd be this happy again.

In Asheville proper, sniveling, money-hungry Charlotte Bouknight, Reggi's oldest daughter, and her husband Edwin dream of the day when they'll have access to Ken Jones's money.

Edwin's losses with this investment and that have made cash the king in their house. He needs it to keep pace with his rich lifestyle and make his much younger wife happy.

Having access to Ken Jones's wealth is paramount. With Reggi marrying him, they'll be billionaires soon!

The Detective

To Addie, Riggoti running away was too convenient. The commissioner in Asheville made her close the case, claiming Joseph Riggoti left Miami, apparently to avoid arrest in Elsie Battaglia's murder. She's heading to Miami to find out from Daisy Fuendes, his "hitman," what really happened to him.

She'll know—the cleaners always do.

The Victim

Elsie and her husband Gen retired to Heritage Hills in North Carolina. He changed his name to fit in, changed it to Ken Jones, left the life of organized crime in Chicago behind, and started a new chapter in the Blue Ridge Mountains.

Then *she* paid a visit, and Elsie was no more. Detective Henson pieced together the events from that day in July; two women on the street outside her home, visitors passing through security, a woman walking her dog and staring at her house, cars rolling slowly by.

Elsie was so happy with her husband, before the killer walked down their driveway, smiling, shaking hands, and then violently murdering Elsie, ruining her idyllic life, ending it.

But face it. As Elsie knows, anyone closely connected to Gennarro Battaglia is always in danger.

PROLOGUE

It's February in the piedmont section of North Carolina, the southern Appalachian chain of the Blue Ridge Mountains. It's called the Smoky Mountains for the great clouds that gather and settle around its peaks, feeding the naturally occurring rhododendron and azaleas, the towering pines, the dangerous rivers that converge and spill into the sea hundreds of miles away.

Spring is weeks away. The migratory birds are seen in small numbers still. The black bears are still hiding, sleeping away until food arrives, when the mountains burst with new growth. Things get busy soon. Until then, it's quiet time. The Smokies are preparing for warmer weather, melting ice and snow, nurturing seedlings, feeding the smaller animals. Mother Nature brings her storms, rains and thunder to partner with the elements of the forest, doing her part for the coming spring and summer.

The stark landscapes of leafless trees, brownish undergrowth, eerily silent woodlands, will soon give way to plush and flowering multitudes, sunny skies and rolling hills teeming with wild animals. And the insects, lots of them. It seems there's always one particular pest for each month of the year. Black flies. Mosquitoes. Moths. Hornets. You need to be prepared.

Then there are the hikers. They fill the hotels, the towns, the cities, making the 550-mile Blue Ridge Mountain range more popular than one hundred Superbowls. Oddly, they hardly ever run into each other. The trails are so diverse, the land they cover so vast.

In the Blue Ridge Mountains, you can lose yourself, forget, run away. A thrill grips you when you approach the seemingly unexplored high hills and deep valleys. Danger mingles with excitement.

Killers are on the loose in the mountains. It's not just about animals and the natural order of things. Oftentimes, they don't want to kill. But if they're backed into a corner with no escape, even the most timid of creatures will become threatening and hostile. They'll do what they have to do to survive.

And the most dangerous of all the animals, the most dangerous in the food chain,

Is Man.

CHAPTER 1 DAISY

Feb

No one is you, and that is your superpower.
Unknown

Flying the friendly skies, Adelaide has time to reflect, having put her relationship with Frank on hold, but she doesn't feel it was wrong. It was the right move. She's sure of it. Once things settle, if he's still after her, if he hasn't lost interest or thought she outright rejected him, then they'll both know more and be certain. For now, though, she compartmentalizes Frank. Puts him in a safe place. Where she's headed, there will be no distractions.

The jetliner touches down in Miami mid-day. As she peers out, Addie can see the typical warm Florida weather with blue skies and tall, white clouds. While she's waiting for the gate jetway to be brought over, she stows away her folder with the background information on Daisy Fuendes, Joey Riggoti's cleaner. She had shown the picture of Fuendes to Helen and then to Reggi to see if they recognized her from the day of Elsie Battaglia's killing. If they had, then she'd be heading to Miami to arrest Fuendes, and not just to talk.

She knows Daisy Fuendes is a very capable and dangerous woman. Her file lists her training credentials as Green Beret, and one of the few women to certify for Special Forces. She's in her thirties, and her self-control mirrors her combat training. Oddly, her file didn't list any boyfriends. Maybe she's binary or fluid. Addie breaks a grin. Then she drops it as quickly as it appeared. She needs to be all business with this person, or she herself will end up in the drink. Feeding the fishes, as the mob says.

The passenger in the seat next to her is readying his gear to leave the plane and grumbling about the lack of convenience in air travel these days.

Addie considers she's about the same age as the man. He turns his head to meet her eyes and says, "Taking a plane used to be fun. Remember those days? That's when you didn't have any security and you could get up and walk around the plane. They even had buffet lines in the aisle of the plane to make deli sandwiches."

Addie agrees, "Back in the nineties. Yeah, I was on one plane that flew to Denver that had a spiral staircase. It went from the main cabin to a lounge area where you could get a drink and hang out. It was like a bar you'd find in Manhattan. And when my parents would pay a visit, I would take my dog right to the gate on a leash, to be there to meet them as they came off the plane."

"Well, those days are over," the man finishes and then stands up to join the other passengers, ready to file off.

"Sad," she replies, as they take their carry-ons and disembark.

She doesn't have any checked luggage since this is going to be a quick trip. After retrieving her rental car, Addie heads directly to where Miami P.D. told her she would most likely be able to find Fuendes. Fuendes is the one person who will be able to more clearly tell her where Joey went to and why. As she's driving, she calls MPD to check in. She needs to tell them she's arrived. She's carrying weaponry, and it's important MPD doesn't shoot her as an "unknown." After the call, she opens her carry-on in the seat next to her and takes out the small lockbox. Opening it, she finds her service weapon and her belt holster designed for concealed weapons and ammo.

She's headed to Little Havana. It's just west of downtown and has a lot of bars and nightspots that Fuendes frequents. She's not a celebrity figure and likes to keep a low profile, but she's attractive and likes to have a good time, too. You can't have it both ways. Addie's first stop is Bar Nancy. She exits her rental, stuffs her gun behind her back, and makes for the front door. It's lunchtime, and the restaurant and bar are packed. Showing the bartender her badge, he gives her his full attention, and she shows him the picture of Daisy Fuendes.

"Have you seen Daisy?" she asks, almost barking the question. She's not here to be polite. Some of the people in the bar are the rough kind, and they don't get white glove service from Addie. What they do get is her unnerving glare as she sweeps the crowd, holding the photo up to the man's face.

When her eyes return to the bartender, he simply replies, "Never seen her."

Addie grips the man's hand with her left and twists his thumb backward, which is a) painful and b) hard to get out of. Opposable thumbs have their advantages and disadvantages.

"Look again," Addie says, and then she smiles that fake, sweet smile that says "*please*."

Wincing, he eagerly tells her, "Oh, yeah! Yeah! That's Daisy! She's not here!"

She releases his hand, "If she comes in, have her call me," she tells him, throwing her card on the

9

counter. She walks out, gets into her rental, and hits up the next place, Garcia Cony, where she does the same routine. And then, two more.

She knows she won't find Daisy in the bars she goes to. She also knows she won't have to find Daisy at all.

Daisy Fuendes will find her.

Addie steps from her rental, parked at the curb in front of a fire hydrant, an MPD permit on the dash. Walking to the nearby beach area, she's decided to take an afternoon stroll on the boardwalk. The sunny day is warm, and a breeze coming from the water smells good. Sometimes, she can taste the salty brine as she passes down the walkway under swaying palm trees. Being alone like this isn't a problem for her, it's her private time.

She needs to clear her head. Thoughts of Frank keep creeping into her mind. And she likes it. So, on this little walk, she allows herself to give time to her relationship with him. She put their romance on hold in October because of the distance between them and because his divorce was too recent. This is what she tells herself. But she knows the real reason is she's afraid. Afraid to fall in love with him and then see it all end. Afraid to take that risk. She's forty-six now, and her track record isn't very good. When she started something up with a man before, it would usually end because she was intimidating, or too smart for him, or both.

Frank's not intimidated. And her current problem isn't that she's afraid to fall in love with him. Her current problem is that she already has. It's been four months since she made her decision and told Frank they needed to take a break. Before that day, those three months before were the happiest she had ever been. Their friendship had taken off like a rocket. They liked each other, were kind to each other, and they both felt deep down they had fallen for each other the first time they met at Frank's mother's house. Addie had been canvassing the area in Heritage Hills to put together the events and people on July 18th, the day Elsie Battaglia was murdered. Frank's mother, Reggi, lived nearby to the Joneses'—Battaglia's—home in the same community.

When Frank walked in that day, he shook Addie's proffered hand, and then held it. She couldn't have cared less if he ever gave it back to her. It felt right. He was smashing good-looking with a thin frame and neatly parted brown hair over an angular jawline with dark brown eyes. But it was more than just that. *He's* more than just that. To her.

Frank is the most important person she has ever had in her life. She feels cowardly and cheap for putting "them" on hold. She's a little ashamed she did that, and it hurt him. But she didn't break up with him, despite what he says. The past four months he's gotten extremely pesky, texting her, calling her, sending her love letters. This guy just won't give up. She really didn't expect him to. She believes it's because both of them think of each other as someone who will always be there, and no one else.

She finds herself smiling, then she takes that smile and puts it away for use later. She returns to the business before her. This is dangerous work, no slip-ups allowed.

When she reaches the southern tip of South Beach, she starts northward on the other side, the bay-side, heading for a place she was last September, when she first met Joey Riggoti. Miami Beach Marina. Once she arrives, she opens the office door, waves to the marina girl behind the desk, and introduces herself. The girl remembers her from September, and then answers the question about Joey. She hasn't seen him since Monday. Addie tells her she'll be going to his apartment and the girl gives her the keys.

Addie exits the marina office, walks over to the small gray building overlooking the marina, and ascends the stairs to the second floor. Looking around, the walls are lined with photographs. There are life-size shots of Joey with his family, with presidents, with his yacht club members, one with Joey and a monstrosity of a swordfish.

The maid appears and asks Addie if she'd like any-thing. They remember each other. Addie orders a club soda with lemon and a small plate of fruit.

As the maid begins to exit, Addie asks, "Can you make that *two* sodas?" The maid nods, then goes down the stairs. Addie sits down.

And then she waits.

Addie hears the door open and then quietly shut. Outside to Addie's right, the gulls squeal, boats rock back and forth, and bells ring from buoys as they turn around and around like drunken sailors. There are steps on the stairs which can be lightly heard also. One. Two. Soon, a head rises slowly from the stairwell. When the visitor sees Addie's piercing, green eyes staring at her, she pauses.

"I asked the maid to bring a club soda with lemon for the two of us. And some fruit. Join me?" Addie asks.

She had noticed Daisy earlier, watching her, tail-ing her. Addie knows Fuendes will be careful and play the waiting game. She'll wait until Addie's alone. Addie's also decided to not make it so easy to be cornered. She decided to go to Miami Beach Marina because they'll both be seen. It's familiar territory to Fuendes, since this is Joey's marina. This is his home away from home, this large apart-

Daisy Fuendes puts her knife away and then makes it to the landing on the second floor. She sizes up the woman seated in front of the windows overlooking the marina. She's shapely with curly, long brown hair and attractive features. And those eyes. The cop's not a tall person, Daisy decides. Today, Addie's wearing navy linen drawstring pants and a loose cream-colored, sleeveless blouse. *Those must be her colors*, Daisy thinks, impressed with this unpretentious woman. She knows Addie's not afraid.

As she steps forward, Addie reaches behind herself and pulls her weapon. Fuendes is instantly on guard and begins to draw her knife, preparing to make her throw. She won't be dying today. She has a dozen moves she can make to avoid injury. Before she can bring her arm up, though, Addie places her service weapon on the table to her right.

"Let's make this a friendly discussion," Addie says passively. "It's a beautiful day today. No sense in ruining it."

"I'm not your friend," Daisy replies, "and I'm not giving you an opening by putting my knife down. It's the first rule of training—never give your weapons over."

"Oh, come on, Daisy. Don't be so uptight. I'm not asking for you to give me anything, like your

Benchmade, or that little ankle gun you carry everywhere you go," she says, pointing to Daisy's feet.

Daisy hesitates, scowls, then takes her Benchmade lock knife and gun and puts them on the table furthest away from Addie.

"Fine," she announces in a huff.

They remain staring at each other for a bit. Addie sees a dark-skinned, wiry, black-haired, attractive woman walking toward the seat directly in front of her. She wonders what kind of personality you have to be in the profession Daisy's in. *Everyone has their insecurities; what's hers?* Addie thinks as Daisy takes her seat and becomes settled in.

"I hear you've been twisting a few arms," Daisy says casually, unable to hide her Cubano accent, or maybe she's using it; it's part of her.

"How else was I going to meet you?" Addie returns, laughing.

Daisy is more comfortable now, believing Addie's not here to make life difficult for her. Smacking her lips, she tells Addie, eyes wide, expressing herself, "You know I go to those places a lot. Now, I have some explaining to do. They know what I do for a living, but I still have to make nice in my hometown."

Addie reflects, then replies, "Maybe we should go back together, and I'll apologize myself, personally. That should make things better. They'll see that we're friends. It'll really blow their minds." She's smiling as she makes this offer.

And Daisy is also smiling, "You're funny. What's your name?"

"Henson. Addie Henson. From Asheville P.D."

Pausing, Daisy makes a statement, "You're Helen's friend."

"Yes," Addie answers, knowing she's referring to Helen Richter, another 'cleaner'. They're all part of the same private club, and they back each other up when they have to. If you don't want to be on the mob's radar, you really don't want to be on their radar.

Placing her hand softly on Addie's forearm, Daisy tells her coyly, "Any friend of Helen's is a friend of mine."

Addie likes eye contact, and their gaze is unbroken. "Are you hitting on me, Daisy?" she asks, smiling warmly.

"Maybe," and Daisy actually looks shy.

Addie never considered being with a woman. She's not against it. It just never occurred to her. But, and there's always a but, Frank is in her life. That's what she wants. What she needs. "There's someone else in my life, Daisy, but I appreciate the attention."

Daisy laughs, "I wonder why I said that. Now I know why Helen likes you."

The small talk over, Addie asks, "About Joey. Where did he go?"

"It's not unusual for him to disappear. But this time, he's gone too long," Daisy replies. "I found his family in Peru. Joey's not with them."

"How'd that happen?"

"The older son, Teddy, called me."

"Called you?"

"Sure. They know who I am. That I work for Joey. Joey and I even dated a little. They're worried about him. They're worried over this sudden move. So am I."

Addie pauses, "I'm not satisfied."

Daisy tells her, "Neither am I. And I can prove to you Riggoti didn't kill Elsie Battaglia. So, let me tell you what I did."

And Daisy Fuendes goes into detail about Joey's disappearance. It's a real eye opener for Addie, and when she's done, *and* after Addie's digested all this telling information, she tells Daisy, "I'll make this clear with the MPD. *And*, I'll make good with his kids, too."

Placing her hand on Addie's arm again, and she's not coy about it this time, Daisy quietly offers, "Then it looks like I owe you a favor." She breaks into an eye-raising, mischievous yet engaging look.

Addie purses her lips in a friendly way and puts her hand on Daisy's. Softly, she tells her, "Sometime, maybe."

Then Addie adds, "There is something else, though…"

Daisy looks at her quizzically.

Addie gives her the look she wants. The choice in the look is important, a look of understanding, a look of sympathy, a look of compadre.

Everyone wants the look, Addie knows, as she tells her,

"Maybe you *can* do me a favor…a different *kind* of favor."

And she gives her the look of need, one woman to another. Addie's expression is non-threatening. She needs Daisy and she doesn't have a problem showing it.

She knows Daisy will respond in kind.

CHAPTER 2
COUPLES

Feb

> Just be you and wait for the people who want that. Naval Ravikant

It's late night in Heritage Hills, cold outside, the wind blowing softly, quiet. The homes are spaced conveniently apart as the gated, secured community is very exclusive; available to those that have that almost-blue blood flowing. It's a rich place, and the people who live there love it, isolated against commonplace America. Inside her own home, Reggi Thomas is tossing in her sleep. Afraid, scared, terrified.

Reggi's running, running. Faster and faster. He's after her, her first husband John, and he has a steak fork, long and deadly. She saw him pick it up and start for her, and now she's on the run, filled with terror. He wants to sink it into her back, and she can hear him grunting as he chases her around the house. She begins to scream wildly as he starts to laugh that ugly guttural laugh of a killer. He's drunk, and that's the only thing in her favor as she hears him slip and fall. She hopes he rammed the slender, two-pronged fork into his gut. He deserves it for the beatings he's given her. She pauses for a moment to see if he's indeed dead or not, and she peers around the corner of a door jamb. Suddenly, he's directly in front of her face, and it isn't John Paulson at all. It's Ken Jones, and he's wearing a horrible sneer, the fork in his right hand. He pulls it back to make the plunge deep into her soft flesh, and, with one wild scream, she wakes up, eyes crazy, sweating heavily. Her bedclothes and sheets are dripping, and as she breathes deeply, she slides her feet off the bed. Sitting on the edge, she takes her head in her hands and suddenly regurgitates last night's dinner. She begins to cry.

She knows why this is happening; it's happened before, decades ago. That's when she tried to kill John. She had let herself drift more and more, trying to escape her sad life. John treated her like furniture, using her and beating her depending on his mood and how much he drank. They had three young children, and the role of father didn't play out well for him. He hated it, and he took it out on her with his unusually nasty sexual appetite and his drunken orgies filled with violence. Reggi began to drift inwardly to keep some semblance of life, the white picket fence, alive. It became obsessive, and then it entered her sleep, where nightmares mixed with laughter and gaiety. Then the blackouts started—and she had a doozy. Her husband John lay in front of her, in bed, and he wasn't asleep. He deserved it, she remembers thinking, and suddenly the Memphis Police arrived and arrested her. They took her kids from her and she spent time in a "special" hospital.

And now it's happening again, and she can't stop it, the onslaught of mixed feelings, smiling on the outside and dying on the inside. She needs help. Maybe it's Megan's fault. Of the two girls, Megan's the one she despises most. She doesn't know why, but she dislikes both her daughters, Megan for being defiant, and Charlotte for being stuck up and rich. But Megan's the one she usually focuses her hate on. Every time they talk, there's the dark cloud of loathing hanging over their heads, raining and raining its pestilence, killing what should be a mother-daughter love, turning it into something dark. Last night's phone call with her was just one more stage show for Megan; her pointing out how destitute Reggi is now over her poor money management, spending freely, borrowing more and more, and never able to pay it back. Megan's so disrespectful, rubbing it in so badly Reggi almost hung up on her. She tried to explain and make clear to Megan that it was Joe's fault, her second husband. When he was alive, he insisted on the best hotels, the best cars, the best trips, and then this country club in Heritage Hills —they never should have moved to Heritage Hills. But Megan wouldn't have it and told her mother over and over how Reggi changes factual history to suit her fancy. Reggi's dignity is indestructible, just like what Nancy Sinatra said about her husband Frank. They ended the call after both were satisfied they had gotten their points across—it's a repeat of many past conversations, and it's growing a beard.

She makes her way to the bath and freshens herself up, finding the scrub brush, bucket, and slop towels to clean up her mess, her vomit beside the bed. Afterward, she feels better and decides to have a bite to eat. Heading to the kitchen, she makes herself coffee and a small breakfast of muffin and fruit. When she's halfway through, the phone rings. It's Frank calling from New York, and she excitedly answers it.

"Well, hello, Francis!"

"Hello, Mother," he replies.

"Taking time out of your busy day to call your mom?"

"I just wanted to see how you were doing. And how you and your boyfriend are doing."

Frank's referring to Ken Jones, the man Reggi's telling her family she's been seeing, a lot. "He hasn't asked me to marry him yet, if that's what you mean. And you can stop calling him my boyfriend. I'm a little too old for that, he's not a boy. Guess what?"

"I'll bite, what?" Frank answers, a little bored of the conversation already, and he begins to look over some papers on his desk.

"He wants to meet my children. That would be you, Frank."

"I know who I am, Mom. I'm fine with it." But Frank is a little surprised with this announcement. This means it's getting serious. He can't believe his mother is going to marry someone at the age of seventy-nine. However, she probably needs to, since she's near penniless, and this Ken Jones is told to be very wealthy.

"He told me he'd like to take everyone on the yacht down to Barbados. It has enough sleeping berths for all three of you and your family. What do you think of that?" Frank can hear she's beaming.

"Sounds good, Mom. It does sound like a fun time. Getting everyone together to do something like that. It makes a great memory, Mom. Hey, Mom? Can I tell you a little something?"

"Sure, Frank, what is it?"

"I'm happy for you."

There's a pause, and he waits to hear her response a bit longer. Finally, she tells him, "Thank you."

Reggi believes she deserves to be happy after her ordeal with Joe, his Alzheimer's, and his passing some time ago. That was a long, arduous two years.

She daydreams about her wedding with Ken, when he asks. It'll be the wedding of the decade. No cost will be too high, not with the immense fortune Ken is sitting on. Reggi reflects on all the lavish parties they've been to together, the yacht they bought, the mansion in Naples, the ranch in Wyoming, the pony he gave her, *and* his alcoholism and rehabilitation. She knows she was a big part of that and feels that Ken owes her for helping him change his life. He showers her with gifts, and she refuses them all. She'll continue to do so until they tie the knot. Reggi has her values, and she knows Ken admires her selflessness, strength and core ethics.

Later in the conversation, after they've discussed Barbados to death, talked about the crummy weather in New York's winter month of February, his son Frannie, and if he has seen Frédérica lately, Reggi asks, "And how are you and Adelaide doing? You two start seeing each other again?"

Glumly, Frank answers, "No. But we have been

talking a lot more lately. I think she's ready to see me soon. I'm not pushing it, but she knows I'm there, and that I'm patiently waiting."

"That's smart, Frank, that's the right move, don't push her away," Reggi advises her oldest child. She loves him, and they have a solid relationship, and she only wants what's best for him.

"I tell you, Mom, I am the best pest ever. I am good. And cute. What woman can resist that combination? I'll get her back."

"Good. I could tell the two of you had that certain connection when you met last August," Reggi tells him, remembering when they first met. It was at Reggi's house in Heritage Hills. Adelaide, in her official role as detective with Asheville P.D., was asking all the neighbors about a crime, and Frank happened to be visiting.

"I remember, too, Mom. Listen, I gotta go make the money, talk soon, okay? Love you," he says quickly.

Reggi doesn't want to hang up, but she knows she has to, "Love you, too, bye."

She wants Frank to be happy, like all parents want for their kids. And their grandkids. Of the five of them, Frannie, Connor, Patrick, Haley and Madison—the one she feels closest to is Madison. She confides in her grandmother, and Reggi likes her special bond with Madison, Charlotte's older daughter. She knows Charlotte doesn't quite understand why.

And that's just tough cookies.

Adelaide thinks he might take **Frédérica** back, Frank knows. And, she's worried over being separated by one thousand miles—he in New York, she in Asheville—it all served as a convenient excuse to break up with him. But he visits his family in Asheville too often. That argument won't work, it won't hold up. He knows he's wearing her down. Being a pest has its advantages, and he smiles inwardly.

He quietly considers his mother's situation. He tries not to think about it too much, but he's incredulous that his mother will marry this guy named Ken Jones, who he hasn't even met yet. This is happening too fast. And he thinks her behavior is weird. She's talking to herself, acting things out...marrying Jones at *her* age? What the hell is going on?

His mind slides away from his mother and always returns to Adelaide.

He misses her, that pigheaded cop who can hum the tune to every sit-com, who can't cook, who gets cuter when she's tipsy. She's on his mind almost every waking moment. She's in his dreams, too. He fell for her from the first moment they met at his mother's house in Heritage Hills and they locked eyes. It was an instant connection they both admitted to.

All this drama is annoying.

Back to the business at hand, Frank isn't really that busy, but he's got something he needs to do. That special time of day is arriving soon, and he hopes she's waiting for him. He kind of knows she will be, but you never know. He believes, hopes, she loves him. And she better quit this little game she's playing soon. It's driving him crazy not being able to see Adelaide and not being able to be with her. Over the last four months, he's turned down a lot of offers and blind dates, he's just not interested in anybody else. She answers all of his calls and all of his IM sessions, so what is she waiting for? Frédérica got dumped by her boyfriend and she wanted to come back to Frank. Even with her knockout body and sexual libido dangling before him, he said no. He wasn't interested in her, either. He's very frustrated, but he won't give up and convinces himself that this is how you feel right before the quiet period, as Adelaide likes to call it, is over.

Soon, it's that special time, and he pings her cell.

ft: *'hi'*

ah: *'hi, was waiting for you frankie'*

ft: *'all things good come to she who waits'*

ah: *'ha ha. yer cute'*

ft: *'yer damn right i'm cute … hey listen, i might come down there in a week or so. is hotel henson open?'*

ah: *'hmmmmm, i'd have to give that some thought. would you be bringing bad frank or cute frank?'*

Wow, Frank's thinking, *she's open to the idea.*

ft: *'a little of both'*

ah: *'it does intrigue me'*

ft: *'what are you wearing?'*

ah: *'what?'*

ft: *'what are you wearing adelaide?'*

ah: *'ha ha, you little pig, i'm not going down that road'*

The conversation continues on at length, taking up their mutual lunchtime. Frank's very excited. She's considering seeing him again, and it plays out plainly in her messages. It's been four months since she iced their relationship. Frank's ex-wife didn't pay a return visit to him. She tried, and Frank said no. Addie feels comfortable lifting the wall she put up, but she won't tell him just yet.

They end the session with an agreement to talk over a possible trip down to Asheville for Frank and whether it's time to see each other again. Her last words are,

ah: *'i miss you frank.'*

And she signs off.

CHAPTER 3
DISAPPOINT-
MENT

Feb

If you let your head get too big, it'll break your neck. Elvis Presley

F BI Agent David Juvieux is ready to tell Detective Henson, Addie, that Gennarro Battaglia killed Joey Riggoti. Everyone thinks Riggoti fled Miami to avoid arrest in the very bloody killing of Battaglia's wife, Elsie. Gennarro Battaglia had retired to Heritage Hills golf community just six months earlier. Retired as overboss of the DiCaprio crime Family at the age of seventy-six. Battaglia set up camp in this exclusive, posh, and gated retreat west of Asheville in the Blue Ridge Mountains and changed his name to

Ken Jones, shedding his given name and his nickname "Biggie". He needed to blend in.

He had his new home built into the side of a high mountain valley, costing in the tens of millions. He took a short trip back to Chicago to tidy up some things, but when he returned, he discovered his wife—her battered face caved in, blood and tissue all around, crows and flies feasting on her remains.

But now, with what appears as Riggoti on the run, having disappeared suddenly, the commissioner ordered the case of Elsie Battaglia's murder closed. He needed closure for her influential family in Chicago, and he needed to get the mayor of Asheville off his back. It's a neat and tidy ending, but Juvieux is going to ruin that. He saw Gennarro Battaglia, Alberto Gangi and Michael Seppi meet Riggoti and his bodyguard inside a small home outside Miami. It was recorded. He saw them dump Riggoti's body and ordered Miami P.D. to recover it. Now, he has the evidence he needs to pressure Gennarro and his boys to talk.

"Enjoy your home while you can, Biggie!" Juvieux inwardly taunts. "You'll be my new bitch!"

With what Battaglia has done, killing Riggoti, and with what he knows about the crime scene in Chicago, it'll be months of hard, satisfying work taking the syndicate down. Juvieux's future looks bright, and Biggie's is, well, over!

Now that the case concerning Elsie's death is closed, Biggie can be arrested and the truth exposed; that Riggoti is dead, and not fled. He knows it will mean reopening the case, but that's not his problem. After Addie returns from vacation, he'll tell her.

He liked working with Addie, even though his first impression of Detective Adelaide Henson was that she was a stuck up, snotty witch. He wants to help her, and he wants to arrest Biggie. So, things are falling into place, and the next months and years will bring huge changes.

He's looking forward to it.

His office phone ringing, Juvieux picks it up, and listens. After the brief conversation, David Juvieux cradles it, glances at one of his agents, and sighs. "That was Henson. She's going to reopen the case. I was this close," and holds his right hand up illustrating a pinching gesture, "this close to telling her about Battaglia and his boys Gangi and Seppi killing Riggoti."

"She knows something. Addie went to Miami. She probably knows more than we do. Shit, this is embarrassing," David laments, and he begins pacing.

The agent he had spoken to first suggests, "Maybe she knows something and maybe not, it's out of our hands. Not anything to get sick over."

David replies angrily, to no one in particular, "She met with Joey Riggoti's cleaner, Daisy Fuendes. That's all she would tell me. That and the re-opening of the case. She's meeting with the commissioner and her captain. Today. That was some vacation she took. I don't know how she does it. How'd she find Fuendes anyway!? Addie is totally unafraid. She spent what amounts to thirty-six hours there and came back with enough back-story to reopen the Elsie Battaglia murder case. Shit!"

The agents in the room feel the frustration, disappointment. They all know this will mean extending the assignment to watch Battaglia's sprawling country house, follow him everywhere. Now, they can't openly disclose how Riggoti was killed. It'll interfere with Addie's murder investigation. Murders trump mobsters, *and* money.

Juvieux puts in the call to his regional director in Atlanta, bad news is best delivered quickly. The man answers and he happily greets Juvieux, "Hello David. Been waiting to hear from you. Ready to get started?" He's referring to the operation to net the largest number of organized criminals, ever. They have Battaglia, cold, in Riggoti's death. He and David are expecting Gennarro Battaglia to roll on the Chicago syndicate, on all the Families. It amounts to the most information ever received, and will result in arrests in the hundreds. It's going to be a big operation. The regional director of the Atlanta FBI station is eager to begin planning.

So, David doesn't answer right away, and the director feels impending doom, "What is it David? You're my number one agent. What's happened. Battaglia eat a bullet?"

"It's not that bad John. But the murder case on his wife is being reopened. Detective Henson came away from Miami with some inside information. She's not sharing it with me. She says the case is back on."

"Shit, David. We have to wait," John states, disappointment heard in every word. "We can't even tell the intelligence community at large that we have Riggoti's body. I'll have to make a few lousy phone calls. I think I'll dress it up a little though."

David is quizzical, "Like what?"

"I'll buy us some time. I'll tell the director we have a planning snag, and that the enormity of what we'll act on needs to be better crafted. He usually won't ask me specifics, he's got more on his mind than this one operation. We haven't stumbled yet, in all these years. He'll ask for a more frequent update though."

John continues, "And that's exactly what we'll do, craft a wide operation. Keep the surveillance ongoing of Battaglia's home in Heritage Hills. At the same time, you and I and the regional team will be planning, just like we intended."

"Agreed, John. I'll be in the office in two days. See you then," and Juvieux hears a click, the call is over.

David slams the receiver into the cradle, almost shattering it.

CHAPTER
4 ADDIE

Feb

> I'm a great believer in luck, and I find the harder I work the more I have of it. Thomas Jefferson

Addie pulls up to the stationhouse and parks. She has a lot on her mind. Her partner Rob has been reassigned due to personal issues, dealing with his divorce from wife number three. Addie's real troubles begin after that. Today, she's meeting with the captain and the commissioner about the Elsie Battaglia case. She gave them a heads-up already, and they've made some time for her. They know what she wants, and they're going to resist. But Addie has a plan. Entering the stationhouse, she takes the stairs to the second floor, finds her desk, and gets her papers in order. She saw the captain poke his head out and acknowledge her arrival. The meeting with the two of them is in a few minutes.

Taking her paperwork with her, she heads over to the captain's office where she takes out her cell and makes a call. He's watching her do this, and he knows that she's up to something. And, deftly, she's *wants* him to know that she's up to something. The two leave his office without saying a word to each other and take the elevator to the ninth floor. There, they step out from the elevator and walk to Commissioner Bill Evans's office where they're shown inside.

"Good morning, Commissioner," Addie politely says, greeting him and extending her hand.

"Good morning, Detective. Good morning, Captain."

The greetings made, they all take a seat at the small round table apart from his desk.

"I'll come right to the point, commissioner," Addie says, "I want to reopen the Elsie Battaglia case."

The commissioner looks sideways at Captain Leary and then back to Addie, to whom he replies, "On what grounds do you want to reopen this case?" He knows what she wanted to see him for, he's also prepared. He gets the nagging feeling he's not going to like the outcome of this meeting. But he has ideas.

Addie tells the two of them, "I have solid information that Riggoti did not kill Elsie Battaglia. I have other information that you're going to want to know. It's not good."

And the captain looks at Addie, "And you got this information in the short day and a half of your 'vacation'?"

Addie replies, "Yes."

The two men look at each other, raise their eyebrows and the commissioner tells Addie, "Go on."

Addie explains to the two of them, "The underground is like a club. Only they are privy to certain types of information, and they keep this information tight. If a hit was placed on Elsie and Gennarro Battaglia, then that type of information might be shared between the cleaners, the people that do this sort of thing, but most likely not. A hit was ordered by Anthony Spadaro. Helen Richter was tasked with carrying it out, we know that from our informant, Spadaro's housemaid. When Richter arrived on the scene, Elsie was already dead. Riggoti's cleaner does not know about this hit. Also, I have reason to believe Riggoti is dead. Joseph Riggoti revered Elsie Battaglia. When I questioned him in September, I came away 99.9 percent sure that he was not our man."

At this, the Commissioner interrupts and bluntly

states, "If you're not 100 percent sure, with evidence, then Riggoti is still our man."

"Then why is he dead?"

The commissioner pauses because he doesn't have an answer for her and asks, "How do you know he's dead?"

Addie stands up, walks over to the door, and opens it toward where the commissioner's secretary is seated. She asks someone there to join her.

Addie sits down, back at the table, and waits.

When Daisy Fuendes appears at the doorway, the two men are all eyes. Daisy is a catching figure, muscular and beautiful—and dangerous.

"This is Ms. Daisy Fuendes, she works for Joseph Riggoti," Addie tells them.

"Gentlemen," Daisy says in greeting.

"Ms. Fuendes," the two of them reply quietly. It's some effect she has on them.

Daisy walks toward the table and takes a seat, her deep brown eyes fixating.

The commissioner says to Addie, "Okay, convince me. Let's see the evidence you have."

Addie looks at Daisy and tells her, "You have the floor. Tell them what you told me."

Daisy begins, "Joseph Riggoti is, wired, for lack of a better word. I know all his movements. All the time."

Evans is not impressed, "So he's bugged. It's not evidence he's met his demise."

Daisy, looking at Addie and then the commissioner, says, "I said I have him wired. He himself is wired."

Captain Leary asks, "What do you mean?"

"He's implanted with a chip, a satellite tracking chip." Daisy looks pretty satisfied with herself. Addie looks at Daisy; she's enjoying this.

The commissioner asks, "Where is he?"

Daisy looks a little uncomfortable, "Somewhere in Atlanta."

"What do you mean, 'somewhere'?" Leary asks.

"His implant stopped transmitting," Daisy answers. "Whoever has him found the implant and disabled it. That's a sophisticated move," Daisy tells them, raising her brow.

The commissioner points out, "So you have him wired. It doesn't make him dead."

Daisy's saved the best for last, and she tells the two men, "My tracking of Joey is like a webcam. It stores weeks and weeks of his travels. When he didn't show for a long while, I looked at his whereabouts. One night last week, he disappeared for a short time, late at night. He was off the radar for around thirty minutes. That never happens unless he's under water, or in outer space."

"So he was swimming, diving," the commissioner says skeptically.

Daisy scoffs and smacks her lips, appearing impatient, "Tracking pinpointed him in the Everglades. *Nobody* goes swimming in the Everglades. His body was dumped into the marsh and it resurfaced before it got eaten, recovered by someone. Then it traveled northward the next day, to Atlanta."

"Who did it?" Captain Leary asks.

"I don't know. But he's definitely dead. This is bad news."

Commissioner Evans looks tired. He sees trouble ahead.

Addie looks at the group, "Elsie Battaglia was murdered on July 18th of last year in her Heritage Hills home, her face battered and caved in by someone using a heavy ornamental bowl, which was found beside her. This is a secluded place, with the homes spaced far apart. Still, there are a lot of people that live there, especially at that time of year, golfing, playing tennis, enjoying the club and its restaurant. Outside Battaglia's home, on that day, at the time of the killing, two women saw each other. One is Helen Richter, Anthony Spadaro's hitman. The other we don't know. Another woman was also seen at that time, walking her dog and staring at the house from behind a tree, but she was seen on FBI surveillance on other days before and after. It's safe to conclude she was there on July 18th also. Her name is Reggi Thomas, and she also saw a woman near the Battaglia's home on that day. Both Richter and Thomas are looking at photographs to identify the woman they saw."

Addie puts her hand on the commissioner's shoulder, addressing him by his first name, for the first time, "Bill, I am *your* cop. Joey Riggoti did not kill Elsie Battaglia. I will find Elsie Battaglia's killer, Riggoti's, too. Let me do this, Bill, it's the right thing to do."

Captain Leary is staring at the commissioner, nodding in agreement, "It's the right thing, Bill."

The commissioner looks at Daisy, "Are you sure Riggoti's dead?"

Daisy squarely says, "I'm always sure. You know what I do for a living. I have to be sure."

"I have one last question," he says, "How'd you get that tracking bug in him?"

Daisy knows this will drive it home, so she waits a moment, giving it impact, and, looking at both men, she explains in a voice that carries finality,

"It was his idea."

The commissioner releases a sigh and looks at Addie, "What would you do if you were me?"

Addie's prepared for this, "I'd open a recovery case to find Riggoti's body and conduct the investigation at the same time."

Both her captain, then the commissioner, nod, "That's what we'll do. It keeps the case closed as is...it allows for Riggoti to be found and the identity of the murderer to be made. Good idea."

They open a new case—the recovery of Riggoti. Both men know Addie is going to do whatever she wants. She begins to detail her next moves, and the two men tell her not to bother. Just come back with results.

Addie leaves the stationhouse with Daisy.

Captain Leary, still with Evans, says, "I told you she was going to come back. Like you said a few months ago, she's going to find that bone. The bone Elsie's family wants."

Elsie Battaglia's family, the Griffiths, they're a dog in search of a bone,

And Addie's going to find that bone.

CHAPTER 5
JERICHO

Feb

> I've learned more from pain than I could've
> ever learned from pleasure. Unknown

Biggie Battaglia's doubts fill him. *Did Riggoti not do it? Not kill his wife Elsie?* He knows he's out of control. They practically fried Joey Riggoti alive to make him confess. Biggie's ready to kill anybody to find out. Mete out justice, DiCaprio style. He knows he's a very dangerous person with hundreds, maybe thousands, of killers at his command. Being the retired overboss of the Chicago DiCaprio crime Family has its perks. Still, he knows he failed. He couldn't protect Elsie. He only wants closure for his wife. It's his final farewell. Closure.

He thinks back to that night they tortured Riggoti to make him confess. He thinks about Junior, Michael's machine, and shudders treble up and down his spine. His mind keeps running, replaying the trip to the everglades with Riggoti's body. Michael chopped him up pretty good. It was Gangi's plan.

The DiCaprios had relocated Joey Riggoti's family in order to make him look guilty. They were flown by private jet to South America in the middle of a dark, dark night. The kids, almost all adults now, are used to their father's lifestyle and weren't surprised; just inconvenienced. Their new digs are opulent, which should make the move easier to stomach. And they were told their father would be joining them in a few months. When he doesn't show, they'll just think he changed his mind.

Moving into Heritage Hills, that exclusive golf community east of Asheville, with Elsie turned out to be a bad decision. He had changed his name to Ken Jones to blend in. It worked. But then his past caught up, bringing a killer to his new home. His cherished wife Elsie was butchered. Murdered while he had returned to Chicago. Most likely murdered while he was screwing Jennifer, his goomah. If that's not guilt, then what is?

It haunts him, the memory of his wife Elsie lying in the living room of their new home in Heritage Hills, beaten and bloody. The smell fills his nostrils, her rotting remains chasing him—perhaps forever. Maybe he wants it that way, stench and all, he *wants* to remember all of it. When he returned home after his trip to Chicago last July, he was startled to find a big, black crow flying from the living room to the outside through the open sliding glass doors. Except they weren't open, they were shattered, and he looked down and found a body, the face covered by a swarm of horseflies. It was Elsie. She was unrecognizable, but it was her, fully dressed as if to go out and run errands. He became repulsed and violently ill, making it to the kitchen and regurgitating, then running wildly from the house onto the street. Later, after he settled down, the dark side of himself swelled, becoming the cold, calculating, dangerous man that lives inside. He knows he's a paradox, that you have to be in the business he was in. One side cold, making decisions, taking actions, controlling and deadly. The other side a husband, a friend, a lover, warm and engaging, honest and loyal.

He only lives to serve Elsie now, and he *will* find her killer if it's not Joseph Riggoti. He *will* have his revenge, and closure for his wife. He has his doubts about Riggoti ordering the hit and thinks his judgment was clouded because he thought Riggoti was a nuisance. That was a bad move he made, unlike the characteristic planner he is, always making the right decision. He believes Gangi knows it was wrong to take Riggoti out, but there was no stopping Biggie Battaglia, and Biggie privately curses himself for letting his foolish nature, his anxiety, and boyish impulses take over.

When he met Elsie in grade school, they were so young and instantly developed a liking to each other. As they grew up, each knew it would be hard to stay together, he from the Italian tenements, she from a wealthy Irish family. Biggie remembers well the looks both sets of parents would make when he, Gen and she, Elsie, were together, dating happily, laughing at all his dumb jokes, catching his sly looks at her figure or her fetching new outfit. They were in love before they knew what love was. His saddest days were when she went to college and he had no prospects. And then it happened. Benito DiCaprio's house burned down and he saved Benito's daughter Consuela from being burned along with it. It changed his life, and Elsie's, too. When she returned from college for a visit, she found him working in the DiCaprio business, the legitimate one, and going to college also, paid for by the DiCaprio trust. It made him, suddenly, an undeniable prospect for Elsie's hand in marriage.

He misses Elsie. He remembers meeting her in elementary school, the cute girl with the pig-tails. He can't remember exactly when he fell in love with her. Maybe he's loved her since the beginning of time. A solitary tear makes its way down his cheek, like it always does when thinking about Elsie. He leaves it there.

47

It's all he has left of her.

And now, here he is, a widower. And he is angry. And he is dangerous.

He will have his way.

That's one thing he's used to, getting his way.

And he will have it.

Alberto Gangi calls, and after the usual formalities he gets to it. "Gen, now that the Riggoti sanction is over, I need to tell you what I've been doing after the Michelangelo affair."

Biggie considers what they did; it was the right thing for the Family. "That's two years ago, Al. That's old news. What could you possibly have left to talk about with what we did to that creep?"

"Well, you remember I mailed his wife the insurance policy," Gangi replies, referring to the severed ring finger of the man they threw overboard. That heavy weight and chains keeping him secure in the deep waters of Lake Michigan. Gangi mailed the finger, with the man's wedding ring on it, to the man's wife, so she could collect from the Family the insurance money due her. The Family keeps money aside to ease a wife's anguish over the loss of a husband. It makes the life easier and is fairly standard practice for men in their line of work. The wives always know to expect bad news one day. It's not a surprise.

"Yes," Biggie says. "I remember."

"Well, I've been hitting that up lately, his widow," Gangi tells Gen.

"You dog!" Gen declares loudly.

"Yeah, she didn't miss him anyway. He used to beat her. So, in bed the other night, she told me about it. Then she added 'good riddance.'"

"What made you decide to chase her?" Gen asks.

"She called *me*," he says. "I have to tell you, she's not bad looking. And sex with her is like, out of this world. She has *some* appetite."

Then Gangi adds, "I'm kind of getting bored with the 'revolving door.' Maybe I should settle down."

Biggie then asks, "What about the other one?" referring to his girlfriend in Asheville.

"You think I could keep both?" and he laughs.

Biggie just shakes his head, "No, Al, you can't have both. Not if you want to stay alive. Those two women are familiar with guns. Ms. Coleman *was* a detective, and when she works for me these days, she carries her old service weapon. The other one is a little crazy, from what I hear. I don't want to bury my best friend, Al."

The conversation takes its regular journey, and they decide to have dinner soon, then hang up.

Thinking about the Michelangelo affair brought back a flood of memories. The thoughts surrounding Detective Henson make Biggie smile. He met her last July when she was investigating the murder of Elsie. She looked familiar, and he remembered her from years earlier. She was with her dad, Jericho, in Chicago where he served as a detective. A couple of high-profile crime figures were found dead, and Jericho came to Gen's Italian Club in Chicago around 1988 to question Gennarro Battaglia. He had brought his daughter to see how investigations work, how they play out, and to witness firsthand the goings on and personality of the underworld.

He was almost fingered by Jericho Henson for that double killing, right after he took over the DiCaprio Family. The two guys were at odds with each other over assuming control of the Family after Benito's retirement, and each enlisted Biggie's help, which he gladly gave them. When the time came for making moves, they were both surprised when the Family agreed to support Gen. After the customary threats the two guys made, the Family also agreed to their removal, from earth. Gangi convinced the Family after bringing the two men's capos forward and hearing their agreement. They weren't liked anyway; they were troublemakers.

Gen did the killings himself, and Jericho found circumstantial evidence...and the bodies. Biggie called in all of his favors—judges, senators, cops —to have the bodies disappear. He and Gangi chopped them up and flew them to the four corners of the globe. Plop. Into the seven seas.

The phone rings, and Biggie takes it out of his pocket, stares at it, squinting, then pulls his head back and says out loud to himself, "This is fuckin' strange."

It's Jericho Henson.

"Hello?" Gen answers softly, he still can't believe it.

"Hi, Gen, you haven't been to any of my lectures lately, and I was wondering how you're getting along. It's been a while."

"You will not believe this, but I was just thinking about you. Right now."

"Oh, man. Not the double murder from the eighties, I hope."

"Yup."

"I'll never live that down. I had to move away to get some peace after that. Did you get our con-dolence card Gen? Irene wants to know. We are so sorry, Gen. I feel for you." Jericho is sincere, and Gen can hear it. They may be polar opposites, but they're both men, and they do think a lot alike. It's in his lectures, the criminal and the cop, that they are alike in many ways.

"It means a lot, Jericho," Gen replies.

"Addie will solve your case, Gen. I trained her my-self. Remember, good soup takes time," Jericho ad-vises.

"I hope so," but Gen thinks his way is faster.

"Let's meet up for lunch. Why not come to my next lecture? It's in Nashville. I'll send over the place and time. Then you can tell me how you made those two guys disappear from the morgue."

"You know what? I'll be there, and I'll tell you what you want to know," Gen guarantees.

The two of them end their call with Gen wonder-ing just how much he can confess to Jericho about that medical examiner in Chicago, and the man's gambling problem.

Maybe he'll tell him everything.

Jericho deserves it.

CHAPTER
6 ADDIE

Feb

> You know you're in love when you can't fall asleep because reality is finally better than your dreams. Dr. Seuss

Addie left her apartment, a conflicted soul, confused at times, so many emotions crowding her. Last night, she started cooking, and she hardly ever does that. She's not very good at it, but it's her coping mechanism. It's therapy, and it helps her think. At least she didn't start smoking. That's her other dead end, gotta-have-it coping tool. Last night it was all about Frank. She wants to trust him, wants to be with him, but she has a lot of buts. It's driving her crazy. What's really driving her crazy is that she can't stop thinking about this man. It's interfering with her work. And she likes it. She let it happen, this falling-in-love thing. She knew it was happening, and she let it happen.

Addie's always considered her family worth dying for, fighting for, it's important to her. She wants Frank to be part of it and wonders if he wants that, too. She thinks so. Her thoughts turn to her brother Bill and how poor his health is. He lives in Santa Fe with his family and he's always been ill, or abusing, or abusive, or in jail. That's another sad story, and it makes her mother cry a lot. Bill's her biggest family problem, her biggest fear, his dying. Or is it losing Frank? Addie doesn't want to replace one fear with another, one problem with another. But she's afraid she's fallen in love with him and she can't or won't stop herself.

As she drives to the stationhouse, her thoughts turn to Ellen, her best friend, who she met as a child. Addie considers Ellen to be part of her own family. She met Ellen when her parents joined a bowling league, and Ellen was brought along by her own parents. That was thirty-eight years ago, and, although they lost touch in their twenties, when they reconnected, their friendship remained solid, and it's been that way since, and it'll be like that forever. Can Addie have the same rock-solid relationship with a man, this puzzle, this Frank?

She's working things through, and the closer she gets to making a decision, it's always this—to open her relationship up with Frank and give herself to it. She's wearing herself down. She doesn't see any other outcome, any other way. She won't deny herself. To hell with the hurts and disappointments. She's a risk-taker, and she wants to take this risk. It doesn't hurt that he's handsome *and* a gentleman. Strong and quiet and funny and even, maybe, romantic.

She remembers last night. After talking with Juvieux she got the distinct feeling he knows something, but can't tell her. That ticks her off, but it's how the game is played.

She was making chicken marsala, which turned out to be slightly burned white meat with something that looked like poorly treated mushrooms. It tasted great, even if it was bad, because she made it. The low calorie count meant she could eat a lot of it, and she did. She tried watching television, but she couldn't concentrate, her thoughts drifting and landing in her personal zone. After a while, she turned it off and picked up what she was reading at the time, *The Last Mrs. Parrish*, which was beginning to show how devious and underhanded people can be towards each other, assuming personalities, deceiving, and lying.

After she started reading, Frank texted her. She dropped the book so fast it fell onto her foot. Wincing with pain, she snatched her phone.

ft: *'adelaide, i know you're there. please answer me'*

She did. They talked with each other over the message thread for hours. As she's driving, she remembers a few clips that keep replaying in her mind.

ah: *'what's important to you frank'*

ft: *'respect, love, honesty,'* he says, *'you?'*

ah: *'family, and if it's one thing i've learned it's to kick toxic people to the curb'*

ft: *'i agree, my biggest lesson i learned is to keep my mouth shut'*

ah: *'i have a confession to make, please don't laugh, i didn't have sex until 24, does that make me a prude?'*

ft: He knows she's teasing him, but she probably was 24, it's not that unusual, she really wants to know if he thinks she's a prude, *'you're the cutest prude I ever met … i was 16'*

ah: *'wow'*

ft: *- 'I also have a confession, ready? I like meatloaf, it's embarrassing'*

ah: *'ha ha, my favorite film is goldfinger, you know, pussy galore, odd job'*

ft: *'mine is little big man with dustin hoffman'*

ah: *'i'll have to watch that'*

ft: *'why don't we watch both together'*

ah: *'down big boy'*

ft: *'why did you break up with me'*

ah: *'i didn't break up with you, stop saying that, i need to know for sure, i'm processing a lot of emotions, don't want to be hurt'*

ft: *'i won't hurt you'*

ah: *'you don't know that'*

ft: *'you're right, i can't tell the future, but i can tell you my convictions'*

ah: *'which are'*

ft: *'one is to not become a bum like my father'*

ah: *'reggi's husband?'*

ft: *'he's not my natural father, my father was a drunk, he killed someone with his car in tennessee'*

ah: *'oh, that's bad'*

ft: *'he died a while ago, complications from alcohol, i really didn't know him, my mother left him'*

ah: *'i'm sorry'*

ft: *'don't pity me girlie, just want you to know i have strong feelings for ideas, people, people like you'*

ah: *'have you been drinking?'*

ft: *'no but i'm gonna start right now'*

ah: *'ha ha ha, you're cute'*

ft: *'yer damn right im cute'*

ah: *'gnite frankie'*

ft: *'gnite adelaide'*

She put her phone down, thinking, *I thought he was going to tell me he loves me.*

And he's still cute.

Pulling into the stationhouse parking lot, she makes up her mind about Frank, to see him again, and she'll tell him the next time he pings her.

The quiet period is over.

CHAPTER 7 REGGI

Feb

You can't blame gravity for falling in love.
Albert Einstein

R eggi slowly opens her eyes. It's morning in Heritage Hills. Outside the wind is softly making its way down the hilltops and valleys, rushing cold, chilly winter air downward. Reggi's reluctant to leave the warmth of her blankets. It's cold in her room, she likes it that way, the way she sleeps. She leaves a crack in her bedroom window to let the outside pour in. She always does.

She's refreshed, she's been a good sleeper since she was a baby. She leaves her warm bed and quickly dons her winter housecoat, thick and patterned, full length and light pink with a floral pattern more strongly colored, then makes her way to the master bath to freshen up a bit.

Reggi notices the quiet as she leaves the bath and enters the kitchen to make morning coffee. Turning the television on to hear the news program, and bring some chatter into the house, she decides to have a breakfast, before she showers, of eggs and toast. But before that, the thermostat needs raising as she takes a cup of coffee over to her breakfast bar.

Looking outside over her rear deck, it's a sunny day and after warming up the cold will give way to warmer temps. She sees her throw lying over the family room chair. When she arrived home last night she was really tired, and didn't bother to hang it up. She paints the picture as she recalls the memory of the night before, with Ken. She imagines he had taken her, rather his driver had taken them, to a dinner dance, so he could show her off and mingle with the elite inside Asheville. The mayor, other dignitaries, the wealthy crème de la crème, even the governor, and a smattering of other minor politicians would have been there.

She begins to reflect on her life and the changes that her relationship with Ken will soon bring. Things will be different when Ken and she marry. Reggi asks herself how she would manage the vast estate Ken owns and the active life he runs. Properties, artwork, board meetings, investments, enormous cash holdings. It's overwhelming for just a girl from Summit, Mississippi. But she'll bravely rise to meet the tasks. Ken will be as proud of her as he will be privileged to just be with her.

Reggi knows Ken wanted her to stay the night. She remembers him holding her tightly, kissing her neck, whispering.

Then she strongly took his hands from her waist and made that stare that said *take me home*.

She almost gave in to his romantic longing. But, she's a lady. And this is how it must be.

When her concentration returns she finds she's spilled her coffee. Her hands are shaking. Her eyes are tearing.

She heads to the master bath again, not bothering to eat, and suddenly feels very tired. Once inside the bath the woman staring back from the mirror looks a mess. Her hair in disarray. She looks horrible. "Who would want you she says," then louder, then screaming it "Who? Who would want YOU!?"

Stopping, she stares at herself a while. Then a smile cracks her lips.

Life with Ken is going to be wonderful.

She turns the shower on, still smiling.

CHAPTER 8 EDWIN

Feb

> Smooth seas do not make skillful sailors. African proverb

His cell is ringing, and as Frank fishes it from his pocket, he looks down and sees his brother-in-law is calling through. He hardly hears from him, so it must be pretty important. Frank doesn't have a bad relationship with Charlotte and Ed, and when they're together, it's natural and easy going; they just don't talk a lot. Frank talks to his other sister, Megan, almost every other day. They take vacations together, and his son and her sons are close because of the time they spend together. Edwin and Charlotte's daughters hardly know their cousins. Frank hasn't even seen their older girl Madison in six years, and

Frank must have been in Asheville fifty times over that period.

He answers the call, "Ed, hi, how are things, girls ok?" Frank asks.

"They're good, thanks." He coughs a little. Frank can hear him wheezing a bit. He sounds out of breath. Edwin isn't well, but he continues to eat and drink like a college boy. He never outgrew bad habits, and they're coming home to punish him. "Frank, Reggi has, apparently, been away for six weeks traveling—Denver, San Francisco, Naples, Wyoming—with Ken. She told me he gave her a pony and stabled it at the ranch in Wyoming, named it Princess. You get that? Your octogenarian mother has a pony. She tells me his ranch there in Wyoming is awesome after it snows. She invited Charlotte and me to vacation there soon."

Frank considers the amount of time she's been out of touch. He's made a few calls, but she doesn't answer, and she hasn't returned any calls, "Oh, so that's where she's been. I was worried. I don't think any one of us want to have a mother whose decomposing body was found a month after she dies because her kids didn't bother to check up on her. Anyway, I thought it was odd for her to drop off the radar. She didn't answer my phone calls. Nothing. And you know she's been away how?"

"I was worried about her, too. Some business came up near Heritage Hills, so I stopped by there. I had lunch with her a few days ago," Edwin tells Frank, and Frank gets the impression there's more to this story. Ed didn't just call to tell him that.

"And?" Frank says, leading him.

"Reggi tells me Ken's been sober four months now and has asked her to marry him. He asked her during a dinner party with neighbors and friends they hosted together in Florida, in Naples. She showed me the four-carat diamond engagement ring she's wearing on her left hand. Take a look at what I just sent you," Edwin says as he sends Frank a picture of it.

"She claims to have the receipt and that it cost over three hundred thousand. They're having an engagement party in May in Naples. Reggi asked me to fly down early, a few days before the party, for some reason. I don't know what for, but I think she wants me there early, along with Charlotte, for some official business," Edwin says importantly.

Frank is almost throwing up over the pumped-up nature his brother-in-law is in. But he doesn't miss a beat and laughingly tells Edwin, "You and Charlotte are the most official of all. You're probably right. She'll need you both."

"Yes, I think so, too. Charlotte told me Mom called her and asked her opinion on a few evening gowns in the Neiman Marcus catalog. They found, with Charlotte's help, one or two that Reggi would look beautiful in. The next weekend, Ken and Reggi took a trip to Atlanta and went on a shopping spree. Ken helped find that gown and purchased that and two others for the engagement and other holiday parties at their place in Naples. Reggi described the dresses to Charlotte in detail. It's only a matter of time for them to set a wedding date. They'll probably announce it at the engagement party."

Frank is shaking his head over this self-important piece of theater. He keeps mentioning Naples for a reason. Maybe he thinks he'll inherit the place. Frank can't get over what has happened to his sister in the years since college. She's the one he'd chase around in the front yard of their parents' home. The girl with the crazy parties and goofy friends. Charlotte's the poor slob who needed a friend when her first husband divorced her so many years ago. It's sad, what money can do to a person.

There's a pause, and Frank assumes Edwin has something else to unload. He does, and it's a big one. "What is it, Ed? You're holding out on me."

Slowly, Edwin begins, "I don't want to jump to any conclusions about Ken Jones. But here goes. Reggi went with us to a party at Biltmore Forest Country Club. Only myself, Charlotte, and Reggi went; the girls weren't there. We were just making small talk when another member, someone I know but not too well, pulled me aside. So I walked with him out onto the veranda of the clubhouse, the one that overlooks the golf course. It can be private at times, and no one else was there smoking or taking a break from the party inside."

Frank is all ears. Usually you can't take Edwin at his every word, but this could be going somewhere.

Continuing, Edwin tells Frank, "He asked me, almost jokingly, about my eighty-year-old mother-in-law and the reported wedding plans she has. I mean, everyone's talking about it. The guy emphasized *eighty* like it was some number at which you didn't get married any longer, like it's strange to do."

"Well, I told him that it's not so crazy to want to be married at that age and that she wasn't eighty yet. I even went so far as to tell him that Reggi didn't want to be married again, but that her fiancé was insistent," said Edwin, at his most haughty, "I told him she's marrying Ken Jones, a billionaire."

"And you know what he did next, Frank?"

"No, I don't know, Ed, I wasn't there," Frank replies sarcastically. "So you tell me."

"And I will. He just stared at me like I had two heads," Edwin feigns surprise. "After a few moments, the man says 'Really, Ken Jones? Wow. Well, I guess he deserves it. It's nice for him after his wife died.'"

Frank's getting a little bored, and he's determined by now that this story is going nowhere, "That's it, Ed? You called to tell me about some boring conversation you had with a guy at your club?"

Edwin tells Frank, "Wait for it. Wait for it. Here it comes," and Frank is listening again. This had better be good or he's going to give his brother-in-law the dial tone. "So I said to him, 'Cancer's an ugly thing, right?' and the guy is looking at me with two heads again. After a while, I said, 'What is it?' and he says to me 'Cancer? She didn't die from cancer.' Then the guy pauses like he's not sure if I want to know what he's going to say. Then he slowly tells me, emphatically, 'She was murdered.'"

Frank is floored, "What? She was killed? Murdered? What? Are you sure?"

"Yes, I looked into it. I have connections. They confirmed that Ken Jones's wife, Elsie Jones, was murdered in Heritage Hills in July of last year!"

"Get out! Did not happen! Really? Wow!" Frank is just shell shocked. That was big news. His mind is running in every direction, thinking, *Isn't September about the time Mom started to see Ken Jones? The guy works fast! This is surreal!*

Then Edwin drops the really big news on Frank, "There's one more thing, Frank. This is really going to give you more food for thought than you've ever had. If information was money, I'd be a quadrillionaire."

Frank becomes impatient. "Ed, tell me now, or I'll let Charlotte know about your little friends," he says, referring to Edwin's down-low boys club he gets into once in a while. Charlotte already knows Edwin likes the young lads, but Edwin's not the insightful kind, and Charlotte continues playing him. He's her meal ticket.

Edwin gets a little flustered, "Ok, ok, calm down. Ken Jones, well, it isn't his real name."

"Ok, now you're blowing my mind, Ed. You're kidding about all this, right? I mean, Mom marrying Ken Jones, his wife murdered, it's not his real name."

"No. I'm not. I'm not kidding. And then there's one more thing. The guy I spoke to told me that Mr. Jones isn't the nicest of people. That he has a sordid past," Edwin explains. He's really depending on Reggi marrying someone wealthy so he can recover from his losses. Edwin's nearly bankrupt. "Maybe he's turned over a new leaf, but it's a pretty big leaf."

Frank concludes Reggi has some explaining to do, and he is very concerned. His head is swimming and he's wondering where Edwin's going with this, and he says in a sappy voice, "Whatever do you mean, Edwin?"

"Ok, you should sit down, Frank, this next part is going to send you over a cliff. Ken Jones is a retired mobster from Chicago, retired as the head of the

DiCaprio Family. What do you think about that? Anyway, the guy *is* retired. And he's rich. And for whatever reason he likes Reggi. Go figure."

Frank is lost for words. This is not happening. His mother is involved with a gangster? His wife was murdered? What is this guy doing in Heritage Hills? Gangsters retire? Is that even possible? She can't marry that guy. What the hell is going on? Edwin still wants her to marry him? Is he insane?

Then, Frank stops with the questions running through his head and it dawns on him. He's pulling one memory after another, one news clip after another, and he practically screams it, "What the fuck, Ed! The DiCaprio crime Family. Oh, man! Do you know who that is!?"

"I do *now*."

Edwin spells it out for Charlotte's big brother, loudly, dramatically,

"Don Gennarro Battaglia."

CHAPTER 9
FRANNIE

Feb

> We do survive every moment, after all, except the last one. John Updike

Addie hears her cell tinkling her ringtone, the theme from *Dragnet*, and looks over to it from the shower. New York is calling, and she excitedly opens the door and reaches for it, stubbing her toe on the rim as she exits the bath. *Damn!* She dances around a little bit on one foot and holds the phone to her ear as she wraps a towel around herself. "Frank!" she answers. "Hang on a minute, I just got out of the shower and I'm, uh, indisposed." And she puts the phone down, quickly pats herself somewhat dry, puts her robe on, folds the towel over her hair and snatches the cell back up, "Frank, I'm glad you called!" She knows she sounds overly excited to speak to him, but she can't help herself. She's not embarrassed to show how she feels anymore. She wants him to know.

There's a pause on the other end. "Frank?" She's hoping it's not another robo call. They've gotten pretty sophisticated; it's really a nuisance. Then her mind plays detective. Something is wrong, and the voice on the other end replies, "Hello, Detective Henson?"

It's Frank's voice, but why is he so formal? "Yes, this is Detective Henson. Frank, what's going on? You're scaring me." The last message from Frank was over a week ago. They've been texting more and more, and everything was falling into place. This phone call is not normal; something is wrong.

And there is something wrong. "Hi, Detective, this is Frank's son, the other Frank. My dad and I sound alike. Sorry I startled you. I know we haven't spoken before, but I had to call you."

Addie raises her free hand to cover her mouth. Something is terribly wrong, and she can feel her eyes begin to well from growing tears. She's not going to like what he says next, she can feel it. This is bad. This is really bad. "Yes?" she says apprehensively.

Frank Jr. simply blurts it out, "My dad was in a car accident in the city. It happened last night. A woman ran a stop light and hit my dad's car as he was going through the intersection. He was hit on the driver side. The car she was driving was a pretty big SUV. We don't know if she was speeding yet. The cops are investigating still."

"Oh my God. Oh my God," Addie loudly expresses, and she begins to cry. She's sobbing, and what she hears next sends her over the edge.

"Detective, the airbags couldn't save him from being struck." As soon as Frank Jr. tells her this, he knows it's the wrong words at this critical time. But it's too late, and he hears Addie dropping her cell and he can imagine she's fallen to the floor. All he hears is her anguished cries a distant one thousand miles away. "Detective? Detective?" he shouts into her cell, louder and louder.

Slowly, she picks up her phone beside her as she's slumped to the floor, her back against the vanity, and, in her broken voice, asks, "Was he fatally struck, Frank?" The sadness she feels is as audible as her words. She has to ask, but she knows what the answer will be. She hasn't begun to curse herself over her foolishness yet, putting their relationship on hold, but it's definitely coming.

Then Frank Jr. tells her, choosing his words carefully, "I'm sorry, Detective." Addie begins crying again, she can't help it. "The woman that hit my dad didn't survive, but Dad's in the hospital. That's what I meant about the airbags; they couldn't save him from a direct hit on the driver side."

"He's alive," Frank Jr. adds.

Addie almost passes out, dropping her phone again, and she releases a loud crying wail, an emotional discharge of relief, sadness, her head in her hands, convulsing with sobs, a release of bottled energy that comes from within. It's from months of wanting and needing and worrying and apprehension. When she's done, and it takes a while, she reaches for her phone again, "Frank's alive? Oh God! Is he ok? Oh God!"

Frank Jr. wonders if he made a bad decision in calling her. She sounds so small, like a little girl. "Detective, I'm really sorry. There's just no easy way to tell anyone about it. I'm really sorry I upset you. My dad told me a while ago about you and said you were important to him. But that's not the only reason I called you this morning."

Addie's beginning to clear her head more, and she's trying not to cry again. She needs to know how bad it is. It must be bad if his son called her. "Oh shit, shit, shit! How bad is it? Will he live? What do you mean that's not the only reason you called?"

Frank Jr. tells her, "The doctors tell me he's injured from the collision, but his internals are undamaged, and he'll survive. But I have to tell you, Detective, he looks pretty messed up. His left side looks like one big bruise and it's swollen. His cheekbone is fractured, too. His left side of his face is red, his left shoulder is red and bruised, his rib cage on the left is bruised. He's in bad shape."

While Addie takes this in, Frank Jr. continues, "I think he has to have surgery on his shoulder. That's today, in around two hours. The doctors tell me that will relieve him of the pain he's in now, and he'll begin to recover quick. They're not guaranteeing it, but they think he can go home in a few days. They want me to stay with him for a week to help him around the house and keep him from going back to the office."

Addie remembers something, "What was the other reason you called me? You said he told you I was important to him, but that wasn't the only reason."

Frank Jr. replies, "He's delirious, in and out. Sometimes he'll open his eyes, but he has them shut most of the time. I think they gave him a pain-killer or two, before the operation on his shoulder. He sees me when he has a clear moment, but I had a reason to call you right away this morning."

Frank's son tells her the reason, and what he tells her drives the nail home on all the emotions she has for this man, everything she feels for him, her love for him. Slowly, Frank Jr. tells her, in a hushed, serious manner,

"You're the only one he's asking for."

After Addie and Frank Jr. end their call, she puts her robe on and sits down on the toilet seat with her hands before her in her lap, trembling. There are a million thoughts trying to break out of her head, all at once, and they all point an accusing finger at her. How could she have been this careless? This thoughtless? To not have been mature enough to see Frank as he is. A gentle man who has developed feelings for another person, her, Adelaide Elaine Henson.

She pushed him away, played games, hurt him. Hurt herself. It's her fault, this mess. Why is she always so suspicious, this foolish girl? She is so angry with herself she wants to scream. Frank is asking for her, he still wants her, after everything she's done or not done. She begins to cry softly. As the tears begin to flow freely, she begins to sob, sad for herself and for Frank.

She begins to think about the first time they met at Reggi's home. He stared at her and she at him, smiling. And the time he came to see her and they had dinner at that little French place. That weekend was the happiest time in her life that she can remember. He was funny and warm, and a gentleman. They shared thoughts they probably had never shared with anyone else. Things were always natural between them. They shared their first kiss, too. At least she doesn't deny herself the memory of that night.

It's been her nature through her life to build walls, to keep everyone on the other side. And it has to come to an end.

She reaches for her phone again and pulls up her airline app, looking for flights to New York City. Charlotte has the nearest flight, but she can't make it there in time. Greeneville/Spartanburg flights have already departed, as has the Asheville flight. The airport here is small, and only one flight goes out every other day to New York. She has to get there, to the hospital Frank Jr. told her about, New York Presbyterian. She needs to be with Frank, at his side.

Staring at the floor, she makes a decision. This is going to be big, but she's a determined woman and she decides it's time to stop following the rules. It could mean her job.

Addie opens the closet and finds her travel bag. After throwing on casual clothes and stuffing what she needs inside the bag, she grabs her service weapon, shuts the lights off and climbs into her car. On her way out of town, she calls into the stationhouse and tells them she'll be gone for at least four nights. That a friend was in an accident and she needs to be there, and that she'll check in every day.

She's heading to Heritage Hills. When she arrives, she passes through security and takes the now familiar drive to the house she's going to. She pulls down the driveway and jumps out, retrieves her bag, and walks to the front door and knocks.

When Gennarro Battaglia opens his front door, he finds Detective Henson standing there. It wouldn't be all that strange except she has a packed suitcase on rollers, the handle in her hand. "Hello, Detective, are you headed somewhere?"

"I need your jet."

He invites her in, and they take seats on the kitchen stools. Addie tells Gen about Frank and why she needs to be there as soon as she can. She tells him a lot, and she knows she's breaking all the rules. He knows it, too. But her story is compelling.

"And that's why I need it. I have to be there for Frank, and he's having surgery in an hour, and he's calling my name, and I can't wait until tomorrow, and I'm in love with him." She pauses, anguished, "and I never tell anyone things like this, and I know I sound like an idiot. Aren't you going to say anything?"

Gen looks at her, and he remembers how young love felt. He misses his wife Elsie. It's softened him up a little. He breaks into a slight smile. He thinks he should negotiate with this person, make her feel as if she's paying him for this, and not exactly in his debt, to make it easier on her, "And what do you have for me if I agree?"

Addie has her hopes up. She's prepared for this question, "I can't tell you who committed the crime against your wife because I don't know yet, but I can tell you who's behind it. At least, who I think is behind it."

Gen looks at her, and he thinks, *if you can't trust a cop, then who you gonna trust? Especially, this cop.* He knows she's waiting for a decision, and he's not going to make her sweat it out any longer. He reaches into the pocket of the robe he's wearing and pulls out his cell, punches in the number, and, when it's answered, he says,

"I want the jet gassed up and waiting for me in forty minutes at Asheville Regional. I have a guest, a detective, and she's going to Teterboro. Yes, that one, in New Jersey. Then I want a chopper to take her anywhere she has to go. She has carte blanche. Treat her like she's me. Anything she wants. Car service, hotel, food, everything. File the flight plans. She'll tell you more about it when she's in the air. I'll drop her off at the airport myself." He wants to make sure she gets what she needs. He kind of likes her and finds himself thinking, *if I had a daughter...*

Addie steps forward and stretches out her hand to thank Battaglia. Abruptly, he pulls her toward him and embraces her quickly. She's too surprised to respond in kind, or to pull away. He releases her just as quickly, and they look at each other for a moment, the cop and the mobster. They both can give a hard look, but they don't and Addie simply tells him, no games played now,

"Thank you."

CHAPTER 10
REALLY GOOD
FRIENDS

Feb

If I know what love is, it is because of you.
Hermann Hesse

A s they drive to the airport in his SUV, Addie tells Gen she'll reveal who's behind Elsie's murder when she returns. She has to first give a certain someone a heads up of what she's doing. Intrigued, he tells her he's fine with it, inwardly thinking that he got Riggoti anyway, and he was the one. Looking up at the skies briefly, he tells her, "Nice day to travel, Detective. Sun's out. Light wind."

"My name is Addie," she says, looking over to him.

"Ok, Addie, I like it. My really good friends call me Gen. Why don't we be good friends?"

"Ok, Gen. I think I like that, too."

"You worried about your friend Frank? Don't be. His kid thinks the doctors there are thorough and, believe me, they are. New York has the best of the best—doctors, food, nightlife, you name it. You just get there and be with him, that's the best medicine. You."

"Here we are," he announces as they pull up to security, and they drive through to the hangar and the waiting pilots. A young woman is with them, with the aircraft behind them. "Who's the girl?" she asks.

"Daphne is your assistant for the flight and on the ground in New York. You'll call her when you need anything and she'll take care of it, make sure it's one hundred percent what you asked for and one hundred percent on time delivered. While you're in flight, she'll make your meal and serve you drinks if you want. Now listen," he says, "You have to eat, or you'll be no good, so have her make a little something for you. Don't be shy and do what you have to do."

"Ok, Gen." She leaves his company to join the others. As they board, she looks back at him, her new friend, and she smiles and waves. He makes little shooing gestures with his hands, and Addie disappears inside thinking, *life gets weirder and weirder. Who'd have thought?*

Before they lift off, while they're taxiing, Addie reaches out to Helen, "I have to tell Battaglia about Spadaro, that he ordered the hit. I'm on his jet, it's taking me to New York City. Frank was in a bad accident, but he's alive. I haven't told Gen about Spadaro yet. I told him I had to speak with someone first. That would be you."

"Oh, Gen, huh? I suppose he calls you Addie. Isn't that cute. Really good friends now." Addie can almost hear Helen smiling, "I guess we'll all break bread when you get back and jump into bed together."

"I'm sorry if it might make a problem for you, Helen."

"You just worry about Frank, not me. I was getting tired of following him around anyway," Helen replies. "Thanks for the heads up. I'll get out in front of it before it's a problem. I think I know what to do. It might even work more in my favor than you think. I'll tell you about it when I see you next. Have a safe flight, bye."

"Bye." They both hang up, the jet leaves the ground, and she's on her way.

The woman Daphne, seated across from her, asks her what she would like to eat. She can make almost anything after they're airborne. After that, they can make the plans for her stay in New York.

"Mr. Battaglia only has the best services, the best of everything, and we're instructed by him to make sure you have it, too."

"I need a drink," Addie tells her, and they both share a light moment.

Addie steps from the helicopter and is greeted by a hospital staff administrative assistant. Daphne has stayed behind with the pilots. She's arranged the suite Addie will stay in until she returns to Asheville. She's arranged for her limousine and driver and given her charge cards to use for any extras she might need. She's arranged for everything; the helicopter, who'll meet her at the helipad, everything. All Addie has to do is show up.

The hospital staffer leads Addie to the hospital elevator, and they arrive at the third floor. The hospital, located on the Upper East Side, is large, and it's easy to get lost in. There are different colored lines on the floors stretching this way and that, and she and the assistant quickly follow the orange one that leads to the C wing on the third floor. Arriving at the nurse's station, the assistant speaks briefly to them, and they look over at Addie, noticing her badge and service weapon she has sitting in her shoulder holster.

The assistant returns and takes her to a family room where they find Frank Jr. This is where the nurses said he'd be. He's waiting for his dad to return from surgery. He practically leaps out of his chair when he sees Addie, "Damn! How did you get here so fast? I just got off the phone with you like four hours ago!"

"It's a long story. How is your dad? Where is he?" Addie asks.

"He's in surgery, he'll be out soon. His shoulder needed fragments removed, and he needs a pin to keep it together and release the pressure. They'll take it out in six months."

"Ok, then we have a moment or two to meet each other, introduce ourselves." Looking behind Frank Jr., she sees someone else, "Is this your mom Frédérica?"

The woman behind Frank Jr. stands up and holds out her hand, "Bonjour, Mademoiselle Henson, I am pleased to meet you."

Adelaide is not surprised, Frank didn't exaggerate. Frédérica is exotically gorgeous with reddish, wavy hair and full lips and a curvy, voluptuous body. "Hi, Frédérica. I'm pleased to meet you also." She reaches for Frédérica's hand.

The two women look each other over as subtly as one can in close quarters, and Frédérica tells her, "Frannie says his dad talks about you a lot. I see why. I like your gun." She laughs a little, "It appears I have been replaced, finally."

"All Frank does is ask for you, Adelaide," she adds.

"I hope we can be friends," Addie says.

In reply, Frédérica tells her, "Better than that, we will be the best of friends." They release each other's hands. Addie believes she's looking at a changed person. Frédérica is no longer the stuck-up witch she used to be. She's Frannie's mom.

Then she looks over at Frank's son. He looks just like his dad. Tall, with brown hair cut in an executive fashion, parted to one side neatly. His frame is lean, and she sees he's got that musculature that only a man in his twenties would have. "He's a lady killer for sure," she says and catches him looking her over also.

"I'm really happy that you called me, Frank," she says to him.

"Why don't we skip the formalities, Detective. Everyone calls me Frannie. It beats getting confused with my dad all the time." He steps forward to take her hand and embrace her, whispering, "I'm glad you're here." Addie feels him shaking, trembling. She feels Frédérica's hands on both their shoulders, and they open up and share the embrace, becoming emotional during that defining moment.

At that instant, the station nurse pokes her head in through the doorway and announces, "Mr. Thomas is returning to his room in one hour. He's in post-op now."

Addie asks the nurse where they like to order food from and how large the staff is on that floor.

"There are over 50 nurses and aides in the C wing on this floor, it's a small fortune to order in for everyone," the nurse tells her.

Addie pulls her phone out, dials Daphne, and looks over to the nurse and says,

"I have carte blanche."

Frank is taken to 302c, his room, and lifted into bed. Frannie, Frédérica, and Addie arrive shortly after. Addie releases a gasp when she sees him. Frannie wasn't kidding, his father is injured. His left side from his lower ribcage to his cheekbone is red and purple, and he's swollen in places. She's seen worse, but she didn't expect to see it on Frank. Frédérica hands her a tissue, and Addie notices for the first time that the two of them are crying a little, that they're both choked up. They look at each other and, after a pregnant pause, they each issue a silly little laugh. Thankfully, he's asleep, and the three of them find chairs and take a seat, watching and waiting for Frank to open his eyes.

Frédérica looks over at Addie, "How much did Frank tell you about us? If you don't want to talk about what the two of you discuss, it's ok."

Frannie is listening in, trying to be the fly on the wall, and Addie replies after giving her answer some thought, "He told me he met you in France while he was there during his studies. That you had a baby together, married later, and that you moved here a few years after that. He said your divorce was hard on him, and he was sad for a long time. He thought he was going to turn out like his natural father. It worried him. If it wasn't for Frannie, he didn't know how'd he keep grounded. That's pretty much it," Addie tells her, not adding the part about Frédérica cheating on him.

"I don't want him back," Frédérica says, and Addie believes her. "I screwed up, and it's over. But we have our son, and it looks like our family may be growing soon, and I'm fine with that."

Addie doesn't know exactly what she means, and maybe Frédérica knows more than she herself does. She thinks Frédérica's relieved she and Frank have a civil relationship now, and it'll remain that way.

The dialogue and shared experiences the two women engage in are revealing. Neither is holding too much back and at times they share a laugh or two. Even Frannie jumps in once in a while. There's something about having someone close to you that's hurt or sick that makes people speak plainly and honestly.

❖ ❖ ❖

Day turns into night, and suddenly Frank opens his eyes and three fuzzy faces turn toward him. It takes a while to focus, to remember what happened, why he's here, wherever that is. Then it comes to him, the crash, it's why he can't see straight. The truck that hit him from the side. He begins to reach up to feel his cheek and finds that he can't, that his shoulder is bandaged, but he can feel around with his other hand that his torso is bandaged about the rib cage and his left side underneath his arm feels tight and sensitive.

He finishes exploring, thinking, *oh great, half my body is out of commission.* As he opens his mouth to speak, with difficulty, Frannie is suddenly hovering over him, and Frank asks him, "Did the other driver make it?"

Frannie looks into his dad's one good eye and tells him the other person, a woman in her forties, died on impact. Frank digests that and purses his lips and tells his son, "Take my hand and let's say a quick prayer for her." When they're done, he asks, "Am I going to be ok?" Frannie nods quickly, repeatedly, still holding his father's hand.

"I have to tell the nurses you're awake," he says and releases Frank's hand, but before he can turn, a voice behind him tells the two of them that Frannie's mom has already left the room to find the nurse and tell her.

Frank tries to lift his head to see the person that said that, but Frannie's in the way, and, as Frannie moves aside, Frank can make out the outline of a woman. As the woman steps closer to the bed he's lying in, he hears her crying softly, but he still can't see clearly. Her hands are close to her face, and he can hear her trying to regain control, keep some composure. As she nears, he can make out her face, see her gun. He raises his hand to his mouth, pointing to it, and says, "This is me smiling."

Addie lets go and cries loudly, putting her hands on Frank and placing her head sideways on his chest, sobbing uncontrollably, "I was so worried. Oh God, Frank. I was so worried. I thought I had lost you. Oh God," words are flowing between sobs and gulps of air and wiping her nose, "I'm a mess. Oh God, Frank," He wraps his arm around her and holds her tight.

"You're not going to lose me, Adelaide. You're never getting rid of me. Just stay like this for a while, it's making me feel better." Frannie hears his cue and brings a chair closer for Addie to sit in, then steps back to make a mental picture of what he sees. It's a painting, a woman sitting, her arms and head resting sideways on a man's chest. He in a hospital bed, bandaged, his arm draped over the woman's shoulders, both staring straight ahead in different directions, the stark fluorescent light behind and above, monitors chirping and small lights blinking, a dark winter night.

And it begins to snow.

Frank falls back to sleep. Soon after, Frannie tells Addie he's going home for the night. He's driving his mom home, too. Addie walks them out and bids farewell. She returns to Frank's room, and hours pass by.

He wakes up. It's early, around four, and she's there, asleep in the chair beside his bed. He sees better now, and, as he places his hand on her head, stroking her hair, she wakes up and looks at him. "Hi, Adelaide. I'm not in much pain anymore. Looks like the doctors were right. I guess I needed a little work to relieve the pressure on my shoulder. Now it's just a matter of healing." Looking down, he tells her, "I feel bad about the woman that died."

He continues, "I remember Frannie told me he called you. He said you cried a lot."

She rises from the chair and sits on the bed, on his right, "When he called, I thought it was you. You can tell he's your son alright. He sounds exactly like you." She looks straight into his eyes, "Frank, when I thought I lost you, my whole world was destroyed. I've been denying myself, you, running away, pushing you away. I was…am…angry with myself for doing that. On the way here I felt so much shame at the way I acted."

He tells her about his frame of mind the last few months, how confused and sad he was.

"And it's over now? It won't happen again?" he asks.

Guiltily, she shakes her head.

They talk extensively about her parents. He wants to meet them. They talk about his sisters who they haven't talked about much. She asks what Joe was like. She tells him about her job as a detective, with a possible promotion to captain. They talk about their feelings for each other, about other people. Frank doesn't like that many people. He doesn't dislike them, just that he's indifferent towards them. He likes interesting, intelligent, active people—she finds that she feels the same way. Each has a limited number of friends. He plays tennis, and maybe she should pick it up. He could teach her. She knows where he's going with that, putting his arms around her to help with her "swing," and what's wrong with that? he asks, and she tells him "nothing." It'll be fun, she says, but first you have to heal.

"Remember when you told me you don't lie to people you care for?" she asks him, and he nods. "You'd never lie to me, would you?"

"No, not you."

She's in all the way, the door has opened.

"I love you, Frank."

"I've loved you since I met you," he says.

They study each other for a moment. This is going to be big, they can both feel it.

"Marry me, Adelaide."

With a look of understanding, she bluntly says, "We don't know each other well enough, silly."

"I won't let you pull that one. I think I know you pretty good," he declares, "You like to laugh, but don't have enough chances to."

She nods.

"One of the reasons you haven't met the right guy is that there aren't that many suitable men that are as smart as you are."

She nods.

"Once you meet someone you like, you dumb yourself down. But the real you comes out, and they're intimidated and they run away."

She hides her face and nods.

"I won't run away," he promises.

After a moment, she looks at him with teary eyes, smiles, and says, "I'll think about it," kissing him on the right side of his lips.

Before she can say anything else, he reaches over to the table beside him. "I have something to show you," he says, and, from the drawer, he pulls out what looks like a ring. "I made this from my bandages while you were sleeping next to me." He takes her hand in his and brings her closer. "Hold it right there," and he slips the cloth ring onto her finger.

She looks at the ring, then looks at Frank. She pauses briefly, staring at the man in the hospital bed on this cold winter night and makes her mind up, "I thought about it. The answer is yes. I will marry you."

She starts for the door and goes to the nurse's station. As the nurse looks up, Addie tells her, "I need some alone time with the patient in 302c, he just asked me to marry him."

The nurse studies her for a moment, then sees her badge and service weapon. She looks at the clock. She combs through her records and finds the information about 302C, Thomas, Frank. She reads the file and reviews it carefully. After a few minutes, she turns back to Addie, looking up at her. "You have forty minutes, stay away from his upper left side torso, contusions, surgery."

Addie nods in agreement and begins to return to Frank.

"I guess you said yes," the nurse asks.

She looks over her shoulder, smiling, laughing, "You're damn right I did," and she holds her left hand up to show the nurse her new ring.

Addie returns to the room and the nurse tells the other desk nurse to monitor the vitals of 302c; they both share a knowing moment.

Addie enters the room, locks the door, and his eyes widen, "What are you doing?"

Stepping ever closer to the bed, Addie begins to unbutton her blouse.

CHAPTER 11
FRANK AND
ADDIE

Three days later

> I wish I had done everything on Earth with you. The Great Gatsby

Frank is recovering, seated in a chair beside his bed, performing some light stretches, as he's been taught. His nurse is in the room with him discussing his vitals and his recovery. He's to report to physical therapy on Monday. The nurse discusses the planned rehabilitation so that Frank is aware and on board with what he needs to do. She makes it clear that the recovery is largely based on his rehabilitation, which they're starting quickly in order to prevent his shoulder from seizing.

Addie walks into room 302c and sees Frank sitting in the chair, walks over to him, and kisses him. Her eyes are twinkling and she's wearing a smart new outfit. She tells him it came from Saks and that Daphne helped pick it out, "You like?" He nods in agreement. New York seems to suit her.

Addie looks around the room and sees Frannie. He's there with a young lady. Looking at the two of them, she makes a guess, "This must be your fiancé, Frannie." He steps forward to give Addie a short embrace. Afterward, she turns to the young girl, "I'm Adelaide Henson, Frank's fiancé. I'm still trying to get over the novelty of saying it. Let me congratulate you on your engagement to Frannie. Do you think we should have a double wedding?" and, laughingly, feeling goofy, she adds, "Just kidding. Frank and I haven't even begun to make our plans."

Frannie introduces her, "This is my special someone, Agatha Winslow," and the pretty girl steps forward, holding out her hand.

"Hi, Ms. Henson, I mean Detective. Pleased to finally meet you."

Addie takes her hand and pulls her closer, embracing her, "I'm not really a handshake type of girl." And when they separate, each feels the other is at ease, the way it should be.

Frank is taking all this in, privately thinking, *so far so good*, and suggests to Adelaide, "Maybe we should begin to make plans for my post-rehab stint. I'd like to come down to Asheville in April for an extended visit. I could stay with my mother if you don't have the room."

Addie turns from her embrace with Agatha, looks at Frank judgingly, then turns back to her again and pans, "You sure you really want one of these guys? I'm having second thoughts myself." They laugh a little. Frank and Frannie are all grins.

Frédérica soon arrives, and with her is Reggi, who is trying to take over Frank's care like any mother, but she's getting shot down and has stepped aside for Adelaide. Frank calls out to them, "Hi, girls. I think it's time for my discharge, I'm ready." The nurse that's been working in the room brings a wheelchair closer to where Frank is seated and points to it while eyeing Frank. Frank gets the idea fully and he transfers over to it. Everyone gathers up what they can carry, and they follow Frank, with Addie walking alongside the nurse behind him.

The nurse, while pushing the chair along, speaks to Addie, "He's a strong man, and his recovery will be quick since he exercises a lot and he's in shape. Still, everyone recovers at their own pace, and it *is* February. We're in the middle of a polar vortex, so it's really cold out. He needs to make sure he doesn't catch a cold, and especially the flu. So, no matter how strong he is, something like that is decimating. He may feel fine, but he has to be careful. Last words," and she smiles without lecturing.

When they're finished wheeling him through the hospital, they arrive at the limousine, and, even though they're in a sheltered exit, it's bitterly cold. So cold the snow won't stick to any surface. But the sun is out, and there's no wind. Frank is told to enter first, and, reluctantly, he awkwardly steps over the door sill and slides inside. The rest of them, ladies first, follow quickly to escape the cold, and when Frannie enters, he looks like an ice cube. His hair is blown around, and his eyes are wet and wide.

In the limo, and as they drive to his brownstone, Frank thanks Frédérica for caring. He's humbled. She replies, "We *were* married. Despite all our history, I think we still care for each other." Then, looking over at Addie, she pauses and tells her, "Good luck." They all find themselves laughing, but it's the relief from potential tragedy that guarantees the release, the laughing, so easy. Frank Thomas was lucky.

After they arrive at Frank and Frannie's home, they bring all his belongings in; the medicine, the therapy gear, the brace, the pulley and cable works for exercising. Frédérica bids farewell, and Addie tells her driver to take Frédérica where she needs to go. The driver tells her, "I'll return after, ok?" and she nods. Looking over at Frank, she tells him the driver won't go home and is always within earshot when she needs him. "I can't get rid of him. He's probably got a hotel room nearby. Daphne took care of it, I'm sure. He usually knocks off around ten, unless I ask him to remain, but he won't go until then, no matter what I say."

Frank suggests Addie look around while he settles in and makes a few calls. Addie raises a brow and warns him, "Nothing too much. Don't raise your blood pressure."

Frannie assures her, "I'll stay with him. Since he's been sidelined, I've been running things. I'll just bring dad up to date and make sure he takes it easy."

"I'll show you around, Addie," Agatha says, and the two girls leave their company after Addie shoots Frank her "behave yourself" look.

Walking through the three-story home, to Addie, or anyone, it's really something. The brownstone sits off Central Park on the Upper West Side. Each floor sports high ceilings with ornate copper tiles and panels. Facing forward on each floor are large, bowed, blown-glass windows overlooking the street below, sunlight filling them. One, a master bedroom on the third floor, the other, a living room on the second floor, the last, a den on the first. The rear of each floor overlooks a private courtyard. In the basement is an apartment that's self-contained with its own entrance. Frank keeps a home office there also, and its walls are lined with bookcases.

"Impressive?" Agatha asks.

Addie says, simply, "Yes. I think I fell in love with the right guy."

Smiling, Agatha concurs, "Me, too."

"Where do you think you'll live after you're married?" Addie asks.

"Here. Frank gave us the apartment in the basement. We can save for a place of our own that way." Then quickly, she asks, "We're not intruding are we? On you and Frank?"

Addie responds in kind, "Of course not. I'm not the pretentious female I look like. I'm a detective, not much bothers me. Except for Frank," she playfully adds. "We don't even know where we're going to make our home. We haven't discussed it. I just said yes three days ago. Look, I'm wearing an engagement ring made from a bandage!"

After heading upstairs, they find the boys. Frannie tells Addie and his dad that he and Agatha need to step out for a while, and they make their farewell embraces. After they've left, Frank proposes, "Let's go out for a walk tomorrow. It'll be warmer, and exercise will be good for me."

Addie looks him over, "But not too much. Now I've read the rehab instructions, your shoulder brace, and your daily exercise routine, and we've got some work to do, but first this." She leans toward him with a warm embrace and kiss, and he remembers the monitors beeping loudly that certain early, early morning in the hospital.

It's his move.

The next day, Addie looks over at Frank while they're sharing a light breakfast of fruit and yogurt. "Today, let's start with a sponge bath," and they head upstairs later, towards the bath. She draws the water and he removes his brace tenderly. There's still a little blood seepage from the incision, and she applies antiseptic and helps him ease into the water. After a few moments, while soaping his back and moving to the front, she teasingly asks, "Francis, are you shy? You devil."

"I haven't had one of these since I was six," he sheepishly replies, snickering.

Afterward, she helps him dress, and when she herself is also ready, they go out for a walk midmorning. Even though it's February, the sunlight is bright and warm. Addie takes in all she sees. At street level is a theater or two, retail shopping, restaurants, corner markets and delis. The street is crowded with cars and buses, taxis, and private car services. Subway entrances are nearby, and the scene is loud at times. "It gets quiet later," Frank says, reading her mind.

As they walk, Frank asks Addie, "I need to tell you

something, and ask you something. Would it be ok?"

Keenly interested, she nods her head, and he inquires, "What's your big casework about?"

She looks at him and hesitates before answering, then tells him, "I can't discuss it, but I can tell you that it's an investigation into a crime in Heritage Hills last July."

Frank explains his elderly mother's fragile circumstances, "And you have my mother helping you with this? She's a witness?"

"Yes, she saw something on the day the crime was committed. I'm not sure, but she may be helpful. We have to follow all our leads to solve the case. It's a big case. It's a big deal."

He dwells on this a moment and mentions his deceased father, to Alzheimer's, "You're aware of how my dad died a while ago? Then there's her own age. She's easily upset."

"I am aware. I'm really careful when I engage Reggi," she says reassuringly.

Then Frank drops a bomb, "She recently became engaged to some guy named Ken Jones. I haven't met him yet. It's happening quickly. I think they want to marry in the fall."

Addie stops dead in her tracks. Frank stops too, and, facing her, puts his hands on her hips and says with an air of bewilderment, "I know. Me, too.

Everyone's getting married, and the least likely are these two senior citizens. It's a crazy world." Then, gauging Adelaide's reaction, he curiously asks, "What is it?"

"I'm just surprised, that's all," Addie replies after regrouping, and her mind is coming to some awful conclusions.

Detective Henson concludes Jones (he was away) and possibly Reggi (she wasn't away, but the idea is ridiculous) killed his wife—as they're having an affair. This is crazy.

Because of the timeline, and after what Edwin told him, Frank believes Henson is investigating Mrs. Jones's murder and that she's holding back.

But for now, they both leave it be.

The next day is warmer, and Addie's driver takes them to 47th St. and Broadway. Addie's still wearing the bandage ring and she tells Frank, "I'll never take it off." They're laughing and holding hands, walking slowly because of his injuries, to the shops between 6th and 5th—jewelry row, the Diamond District. He suggested they go early to avoid crowds. He doesn't want to physically bump shoulders with anyone. She'll pick out her setting and stone today.

They're enjoying shopping around and are both excited over their engagement. After looking over the inventory at a number of dealers, Frank suggests they go to a high floor where specialty dealers are, inside a building across the street. She selects a setting at a dealer Frank has known for a number of years.

The dealer, Samuel his name, suggests they interweave the cloth inside yellow 24k gold. The couple will be able to see the outlines and imperfections the bandage introduces to the setting, and there will never be another like it. It will last forever. It's a very compelling design to go with a likewise compelling story behind it. They instantly warm to the idea, smiling broadly, and the dealer imagines he's with a couple of teenagers.

The setting they choose is a high mount, and the stone is a three carat, near perfect, teardrop, pear shape. It's just right. The dealer tells them the price, one hundred thousand dollars. Disappointed, Addie suggests to Frank they downsize. Frank looks at Adelaide and tells her, "I'm not buying another one ever, ever. Let me see what we can work out." Looking over to the dealer, he asks, "What's it really worth, Samuel?"

Addie takes this as her cue and tells the two of them she needs to go to the powder room. After the door closes, Frank begins the bargaining, the dance, "I think forty."

Samuel looks hurt, "This is artisanship, you can't just buy that. This will be art!"

"Sixty," Frank says.

"Ninety," the dealer says.

"I'll meet you in the middle."

"Done."

After Addie returns, Frank asks her to remove the bandage ring she has on, and she does. Looking at her finger now, she feels somewhat lost without the ring of cotton on her left hand. Frank slyly notices her expression.

Frank shakes hands with Samuel and they leave the dealer, bidding farewell to him. He told them the ring will be ready in a month, with papers. Leaving the Diamond District, they walk over to have lunch at Rockefeller Center, in the restaurant that looks out at the skating rink, the Rock Center Café. It's very romantic, having a light lunch and watching couples skating, laughing. Every once in awhile, someone will lose their footing and slip, landing on their rear end. Conspiratorially, they look at each other, amused.

After lunch, Frank takes Addie to the Peninsula Hotel on 55th, where they take a private elevator to the top, to the rooftop lounge. Here they can look over the city, over Fifth Avenue. Frank tells her, "This is one of my favorite places. Where else would you find these views and thirty-dollar beers." They share an amusing, muted laugh that only couples in love can, looking into each other's eyes.

He takes her to the side of the roof, looking north, up Fifth Avenue. The street scene is very busy. This is the media area of Manhattan, and you'll find every cable group, news media, every station, right there. Anything that deals with reaching the public; political figures, foreign powers. It's a big deal, and today is a work day. From the twenty-second floor, the view reaches to Central Park and down to the Empire State Building. It's impressive.

He knows she misses her ring. "I have something for you. I brought you here so we'd remember this," and he brings out a small box from his pocket and gets down on one knee. The other people nearby stop and watch as she slowly opens the box. She stares at the contents and brings her other hand to her mouth, trying not to cry. Inside is another cloth ring, made from his bandage. "I made this for you last night, Adelaide, while you were sleeping. Will you marry me?"

The tears begin to flow, "Yes, I will marry you." She leans down closer to him and whispers into his ear, as loudly as one can without being heard by anyone else, "Now get up, ya stud, you're embarrassing me."

The rooftop lounge of the Peninsula Hotel erupts

in applause and celebration.

They wake up the next morning well rested. She's looking at him, "g'morning Frank." He turns toward her, and she brushes the hair from his eyes, "I love you."

They have breakfast together. Addie returns to work that day. He tells her he'll be there in April. "We'll talk every night."

Addie looks him over, "Just finish healing."

Frank sees the detective in Adelaide has returned. She's all business as she packs and then marches out to meet Daphne and the waiting limousine.

CHAPTER 12
REVELATIONS

March

> If I'd observed all the rules, I'd never got any-
> where. Marilyn Monroe

Daphne's making a light lunch on the way back to Asheville. When they left New York, a gentle rain had begun to fall, as an unusual warm front had enveloped the metrop-olis in contrast to the stark, harsh cold weather earlier in the week. Addie found herself lik-ing New York City, and her mind wandered to thoughts of living there with Frank, as her hus-band, in his home on the West Side. Despite the busy, crowded streets, it held an allure for her that she didn't expect. It's more than just an appeal, it's a temptation.

Still, Asheville is where she calls home, and her

life is there. She built it, and it wasn't easy. With Frank, things will be different, and she knows there will be changes and compromises they'll both make, readily. She's in line for promotion to Captain. Closing this case will seal that likelihood. Does she really want to abandon that? Would she make that sacrifice? Where's the middle of the road? It's going to be a bridge they'll cross or build as they go along, but a little guidance can't hurt. They have a lot to talk about. Addie begins to smile as she thinks about their future together.

Looking down at her hand, she spies her ring; a piece of thin, dirty woven bandage wrapped around her finger. What's happened over the last week replays in her mind as Daphne sets the table. First, she lost Frank, then she found Frank alive, then she said yes to marry him. She met his ex-wife Frédérica, and their son Frannie and his fiancé Agatha. She even made love to Frank in the hospital. It was beautiful. "What the hell is happening me?" Addie mulls, "I never..." She silently, meekly lets herself express what might look like a smile, but it's more like a contentment, and Daphne looks at her in the knowing way that one woman has for another.

"Lunch time," Daphne announces, and they both sit down to have a bite together. As they dig into the food before them, the jet continues onward, white, full, almost weightless clouds beneath them, clear skies above. Even with the turbines growling, the journey is serene, and the sooth- ing calm of a week spent in peace and happiness settles in around them. As they share the meal, they begin to learn more about each other, and Daphne's not concerned Addie the Detective will insert herself into the conversation; she's com- fortable.

"It's a strange life we can lead sometimes," Daphne reflects. "First you think you've lost Frank, and the next moment, you're engaged," she observes hap- pily.

Addie can't believe what's happened herself. "I couldn't have predicted this in a million years. I haven't given it much thought, but I wonder how much of a change it's going to be to have a hus- band."

"Oh, wow. That will be big!" Daphne declares. "Having someone else when you wake up, when you get home, have their toothbrush in your bath- room, their clothes in your closet. It's a huge, huge change!"

Addie is becoming a little scared, with trepida- tion and foreboding creeping into her thoughts. "I didn't really consider the reality of everyday life yet, but you're right. Do you think it's fun, to have that change? I mean, it's a major life shift."

Without thinking about it, Daphne tells her, "You will love it. I just know it. Who else wears a ring made from a bloody bandage?" They both share an intimate laugh.

"Do you have a special someone?" Addie asks and waits patiently for Daphne's reply.

After a hesitant moment, Daphne tells her secretively, "I'm seeing Al for a while now. I haven't felt like this about a man in a long time."

Addie asks her, "Al? Who's that? Al who?"

"Al Gangi, Mr. Battaglia's friend."

Addie thinks to herself that she is going to need a lot of therapy to cope with all of these revelations she's been given in the past five days. "You are seeing Gangi, Gennarro's right hand man. You know who he is, right?"

Daphne believes Addie doesn't exactly approve, and she doesn't exactly disapprove. "I know Al was his underboss, yes. When I met Al here, it wasn't the first time I had run into him. I was a police officer in Chicago, and we had our share of run-ins. I retired and came here, and so did he, and we ran into each other again, and the past is the past."

"I'll tell you a little story," Daphne says. "When I first ran into Al here, he thought I was going to arrest him. His eyes were as big as saucers. He tried to hide, so he ducked into a candy store. Picture that: The big, tough Alberto Gangi hiding in a candy store," and they're both laughing. "He came out when he realized he couldn't get away. I was waiting for him and I said 'Hello, Al, what are you doing here?' and he was so scared he couldn't speak, so he flubbed his words and I leaned over to whisper in his ear, 'Remember me? Detective Coleman?' and I think he peed himself a little." The two of them are screeching with laughter, and the pilots, hearing this, just look at each other over this scene they've seen played out before. "Later, we talked after he calmed down and we've been seeing each other for around a year."

"I know he can be a naughty boy, especially when he goes to Chicago. But he's doing that less and less, and I think I know why." Addie looks at her expectantly. Daphne appears soulful as she reaches within, and, looking at Addie, she quietly tells her, "He knows I like him, and that's something he doesn't get anywhere else."

"I think I love him."

Addie is speechless. After a short while she asks, or rather, tells, her, "You were a police officer? In Chicago? And you know Al Gangi? And you're in love with him?"

Daphne nods, reaches behind her, and brings out her service weapon, "Narcotics, undercover. Mr. Battaglia requires everyone that works for him be armed."

Addie looks at it, then back to Daphne, then back to the gun, "No shit."

As the pilot guides the jet close in on the Smoky Mountains, he announces to the girls to take their seats, they'll be landing soon. They sit and buckle themselves in, and each is looking out their tiny windows. The low cloud cover is sliding around peaks dotted with tall pine trees and heavy undergrowth and settling in over valleys. There isn't much traffic today, and it's early yet. The flight from Teterboro is around seventy minutes long, and they touch down at Asheville Regional easily. Once the aircraft arrives at her hangar, Addie looks over to see Gennarro waiting. She's not happy with what she has to do today. She hopes Gen won't be angry with her. But it's her job, and she's probably the best person to tell him. She'll give him a chance to clear things up, but it looks bad. If anyone has to do this, she's the one best suited.

The door is opened by one of the pilots, and, as she hugs Daphne in farewell, she exits through the door and begins to walk down the stair, waving to Gennarro and watching him wave back. "Hi, Gen, thanks for picking me up." They get into his car and leave. Driving to Heritage Hills, Gennarro decides to take surface roads as opposed to the expressway and explains Mother Nature has given them a good weather day and winding roads will mean a longer trip back, but not too much. They'll enjoy the scenery, and it'll give them more time to talk.

His eyes are on the road as he says, "It's nice to see you, Addie. It can be lonely up here sometimes, and it's good, for me anyway, to see a friendly face. I see and talk to neighbors and people at the club, but it's not the same. I'm thinking about leaving Heritage Hills, did I tell you that?" Addie tells him no. "I'm thinking about moving nearer to Al."

"Really? You might like that," Addie replies, adding, "Did you know that Al is seeing someone around here?"

Gen glances her way and smiles, "You mean Daphne? Sure, I know about that. Al and I are like brothers. We know everything about each other. We have no secrets. He told me he likes her, and I see he's spending more time with her. People in our line of work don't find too many others that 'like' us, whether we're retired or not. When we were in Chicago, she served as the arresting officer in cases involving Al around five times. Now we know why. No better way to get close to someone than to arrest them." He lets a quiet chuckle loose.

Then he notices her hand and asks, "What is that?" referring to the bandage ring, "It looks dirty."

Addie manages a broad smile, and, before Gen can remark on how wide it is, she tells him, "Frank asked me to marry him and I said yes. He made a ring out of his surgical dressing, and no, it's not dirty, it's dried blood."

Gen allows a soft whistle to escape slowly and remarks, "That was some trip. Save a guy's life, get engaged, private jet. You have some life, Detective. The gods are smiling on you."

Addie feels the same way, except for what she has to say to him, but she saves it for when they arrive at his home.

Gennarro's satisfied but bothered that he achieved revenge for Elsie. Still, he's sure Riggoti did it, but at times he's not sure Riggoti did it. The confession was extorted from a man who was roasted alive. Riggoti committed a violation of his 'space' by killing his wife, invading his home. The nagging thoughts won't stop, and it's eating away at Gen, but with each day it becomes less and less, and Gen's certain he's just feeling natural remorse. He's human after all.

"Gen, before I left I told you I had information for you, about your wife's murder. Now, this is important, the only ones that know this are my captain and the commissioner." Gen is listening intently, his eyes never leaving the road, and she takes a deep breath, "When I went to Chicago in August, my mission was to speak with around thirty sources. One of the visits I paid was to Anthony Spadaro. By the way, he's a pig."

"I know."

"The FBI are watching his home."

"They watch everyone's home."

She laughs a little. "Anyway, while I was there, I was stopped by someone I didn't expect to talk to. That source told me that Spadaro ordered a job, a hit." She ends by dropping the bomb, "and that job was to have been carried out in July."

He shows no reaction. His wheels are turning inside his head. As they pull down the long driveway and the garage door opens, he mutters under his breath, "That fat prick." Addie knows he's no friend of Anthony Spadaro.

Then Gen speaks out loud, "This means Helen's involved."

"Helen tells me she didn't do the job," Addie says after they've entered the house. "She told me there was someone else there, and we're looking for that person."

"Helen told you this?" Gen is a little confused.

"Yes, she's helping us. I had the goods on her, so she's helping, but we don't have anything solid yet. She tells me she likes doing it, looking at mug shots and stuff."

"*The* Helen?" he asks.

"Yes, we got to know each other. We even went clothes shopping a few times."

"Helen the hitman? Clothes shopping?"

"Yes," she says, emphatically this time.

"Helen Richter?" Gen's just staring at her.

"Yes, we kind of like each other. She told me she's retiring."

Gen shakes his head, as if trying to clear it. "*Wow*... Wow." After coming to grips with this news, he invites Addie to make herself at home. "Please take a seat in the living room, Addie, and I'll make some coffee for us. I can feel you have more to tell me, so let's not rush things. I want you to tell me about your trip," he says as Addie walks by and into the living room.

She's thinking, *He's not wrong about that. I have a lot to tell him.* She reflects on the scene she's a player in at the moment; the detective and the mobster, one of the most dangerous and richest men in the world, making coffee for her.

As he enters the room with a tray of coffee and cookies, she tells him, "I arrived early in Manhattan the day I left here. I am so grateful for your help. I was beside myself, and you helped me. Daphne and the pilots were really nice to me, too. You should have seen Frank's son's face when I walked in. If it wasn't for Frank's accident, his expression would have been hilarious. Frank's ex was there, too. Turns out she's very nice and we became friends."

Pouring coffee, he adds, "That's great; so far so

good."

Continuing, she recalls, "After they brought me up to date, Frank returned from surgery and we went to his room," and she becomes grim, "and he was badly hurt. He was really bruised and banged up. The doctors told us he was devoid of any internal injuries and that he would recover quickly. And he did. We all feel that Frank was very lucky. The person in the other car died."

"Oh, that's bad, I'm sorry."

"There was a lot of crying that day. But he did recover, and we could eat together and take walks, and he proposed the next morning very early from his hospital bed. He made a ring from his bandage and placed it onto my finger. Later in the week, we paid a visit to a dealer in the Diamond District and, well, the ring should be ready in a month."

"I see," Gennarro tells her, "I'm happy for you. You look happy." He pauses, studying her, "You have something else to tell me, and it's not good news."

Addie's a little startled that he can read her emotions and motives from looking at her, but she's not very good at hiding her feelings sometimes. "I have something I learned while I was away. There's really no easy way to tell you this."

He looks confused.

Addie assembles her thoughts and begins, "I learned you are engaged to Reggi Thomas, another resident here." There, she said it. And she looks for his reaction, but he's good, and his poker face is on. "I'm also told you started dating her in September, two months after Elsie was killed."

Still, poker face.

"That you and Reggi have been on trips to Wyoming together, where you have a ranch. And that you gave her a pony."

"That you and she bought a yacht and it's anchored near your newly purchased mansion in Naples. That her name is going to be on the deed after you're married."

Still, poker face.

"Gen, you know how this looks," she pleads. He feels bad for her, she finds telling him these things very unpleasant. "This looks like you had an affair and conspired to take your wife out of the picture. This is how it looks. At best, you used or tricked Reggi into killing her, or having someone kill her." She's practically begging him to tell her a valid reason for all of it.

Inside, his wheels are turning. Who told her about Spadaro? What's this? Who told her about Reggi Thomas?... It happened on her trip?

Addie leads Gen to believe their investigation into the murder of Mrs. Jones has two suspects—him and Spadaro. Everything points that way, and once they have a concrete case, someone will need very good lawyers to defend themselves.

She tells Gen to not leave the area.

Gen is pacing, and while constructively thinking, says, "There is more to the story. You've just started scratching. Something is happening, and you need to dig deeper."

She stares at Gennarro, wondering what he means.

Gen's talking out loud again, "I don't know, but you need to keep digging on this. I wouldn't kill my wife." He tells her about how he met Elsie, the little rich girl with the pigtails and red hair, how he got involved with the DiCaprios. He tells her Elsie agreed to marry him against her family's wishes. He tells Addie how much he loved his wife.

Addie is so confused and twisted. She believes him. She believes also that there is more, somewhere, and resolves to open the investigation up wide. "Ok, Gen, I believe you. Frank tells me that he never lies to people he cares for. I think you see things that way, too. But others from my station will just want to put you away with this evidence."

"I know. I'll tell you something else." Addie looks at him, and he says, "You didn't have to give me Spadaro, although that is very interesting."

He tells her in a friendly way, one man to one woman he feels is someone he can trust,

"I was ready to loan my jet to you anyway, no matter what."

CHAPTER 13
DECISIONS

March

> I've never felt better – Douglas Fairbanks, right before he died.

Gangi terminates the call after speaking to Gen. That was some phone call. That detective friend of his told him Reggi Thomas said she was engaged to Ken Jones. So, Gen wants a complete work-up on Reggi Thomas. Gen tells him her address in Heritage Hills. After writing it down, Gen dropped the next news headline about Spadaro ordering a hit, and the job was supposed to be done in July of last year. That's when Elsie was murdered. Then Gen told him that Helen got the job, but she didn't do it. Gangi's wondering how this friend of his gets all this great information. Someone is dropping things right into

Gen's lap. The news about Spadaro is big, and then Gen told him about the Detective and Helen being friends, and he was blown away. Helen Richter, the nail. He and Gen shared a couple of stories about Helen, especially her younger days, and this is certainly not normal for her, or for the detective.

Gangi calls his boy Roger and gives him the parameters on the work-up. Roger's the guy they use to investigate people. He may be in Chicago, but he does his work remotely anyway, and he's never onsite. Gangi wants Roger to do some deep diving on Reggi Thomas and her family, and her grandchildren. He wants a clear picture of everyone's financials—debt, assets, money made and money lost. He even wants to know about pets. Roger knows how to get this done quickly. He'll use social media and he'll hack their email accounts; nothing is private on the internet anymore.

He wants to know about their affiliations, friends, habits, professions and licenses, arrest history, driving record.

Lastly, Gangi wants the work-up on their medical state and history, medications, and psychiatric specifics, but he can wait on that. Information of this nature takes longer to obtain.

When he's almost done talking to Roger, he hears a knock at his front door. He's a little surprised. Strangers are rare, and where he makes his home, there are no solicitors. It can't be Daphne. He spoke to her this morning and they talked about having dinner out tonight. He decides to not answer the knock and continues on with Roger, giving him the final instructions on when to deliver what, and how rushed some of this is. The knock persists, and now Gangi is annoyed. He walks into the kitchen and over to the video feed from the front door, and what he sees is nerve wracking.

It's Helen Richter, and she bangs on the door again, loudly, and he hears her singing, "Helloooo. Open up, Albertooooo."

"I have to call you back, Roger," and he hangs up without hearing his answer. Before she can knock again, he rushes into his bedroom and opens the nightstand. Taking out his Glock, he stuffs it into his pants, resting in his rear beltline. Peering through his bedroom curtains, he finds Helen staring back at him and he jumps a little, "Hi, Al! It's me, Helen. Open up."

He runs to the front door and pulls his weapon, thinking he almost shot himself as he grabs it. Helen can hear his breathing through the door jamb, and she softly tells him, "I have something to talk to you about. You know, like one person to another. Mano y Mano." She's kind of enjoying this. She knows Gangi believes she's there to kill him. She knows he learned about the Spadaro-ordered hit from Biggie. It's only natural Gangi would be thinking he's on the A list.

"C'mon Al, open up. I have to talk to you," she says laughingly. Al is puzzled, why is she laughing? Helen Richter doesn't laugh, he's never seen her even smile, or crack a grin. "I have an offer for you, Al."

He's thinking, *I'll bet she does. Six feet under, that's her offer*. His mind is trying to put together his options. You can't outrun her, and you can't scare her. He could make a call and get some help, but he'd be dead by the time they showed up. His only choice is to face her on even ground, but he knows his odds are pretty dim. It's the only way. So he asks her nervously through the door, "What do you want, Helen? Why are you here? I'm fuckin' retired. What do you want?!"

"I want to talk to you, that's all. Calm yourself, boyfriend. Take a look through your peephole and I'll show you I'm not armed."

"Yeah, so you can shoot me through the eye. Nice try! Get the fuck away from me!" he shouts.

"Now, now, your neighbors can hear you. You don't want that," she tells him in her best soothing voice. "No one is here to hurt you," and she adds quietly, "You know if I wanted you dead, I wouldn't knock. Let me in, and we can work things out like two adults. And stop your crying and whining. It's unbecoming, and you're embarrassing yourself."

Gangi's a little insulted, humiliated, and scared all

125

at the same time, and he does what any normal sixty-one-year-old man might do, and he begins to open the door, peering through the crack as it becomes wider, waiting for the loud bang of her pistol and the splitting headache as the rear of his head explodes. He finds himself sweating, and he's beginning to smell, and suddenly Helen is standing there and the door is fully open.

She reaches up and pinches his cheek, "Hello, old friend," and smiles at him.

She's seated at his breakfast bar, wearing light khakis and a neat, white blouse, sandals on her feet. She's even wearing lipstick and makeup, and Gangi is a little freaked out. The Helen he knows wouldn't look like this. No, she'd be wearing almost all black, with a severe, pale facial expression, a look of death, and talking in terms of finality. Not the little lady he's picturing here at all, talking about hiking in the Smokies and how good dinner was last night, and that she's developed a taste for okra and collard greens. She tells him about the man she met at the bar and how funny he was. Dancing lightly to country songs and sharing a beer or two, and that the man was a good dancer and they traded phone numbers at the end of the night. Gangi is perplexed, with one thought running through his head, *What is going on here?*

She suggested they have a little coffee together and wouldn't he make some. So he did as he was ordered and poured the grounds into the machine and filled it with water from his sink, all the while keeping her in view so he could at least see his final moments play out as she draws some hidden tool of the trade and watches him die. But it didn't happen, and he places two cups with hot coffee on the counter, grabs some milk and sweetener, and pensively takes a seat beside her. He reaches behind him and, with one hand, still looking at her, he grabs a jar of biscotti. "These are from Chicago, they're authentic. Not the stuff you find around here. These are from the bakers of the old country."

She takes a chocolate one and says, "My favorite, thank you, Al," as she begins to bite small pieces off and sip her coffee. "Coffee's good, too. I didn't know you were such a foodie. It's fun facts like that that keep life worth living," she says, chuckling lightly. Al is definitely weirded out, but he's growing calmer as each minute passes that he's not dead.

"Hey, ever had grits?" he asks. "I make some killer grits with bacon. One small bowl of that will stick to your ribs and you're good all day," he says, surprising himself. This is almost going so good, it can't be real, and he's almost forgotten that he's waiting for the end, a bang, a cut, a stab.

"I have had grits. Not my favorite, but maybe you

127

can change my mind," she says playfully, and he thinks Helen's almost hitting on him. "Gen should see this. It would blow him away." Gangi looks over at Helen and she's smiling at him and they look at each other for a moment and he adds, "I can make some now."

"Sure, why not? Let's have brunch together. I'll make eggs and toast, and you whip up the grits and bacon." He shows her to where he keeps his pans and bread, and they begin to cook together. It is the strangest scene he's been in since, well, forever. Stranger than the hookers and the bizarre S/M costumes. Stranger than Michael and Junior.

Helen knows Al is worried and scared. She would be too if she were him. She has a stellar reputation in the field of elimination. Most of her targets never see her, and their demise is instant. She's not interested in inflicting pain. She also knows that the way to a man's heart is through his stomach, and the best way to calm him down is to eat. Making brunch is just a way to put some of this attention and restless energy into something else besides fear. As they cook side by side, she begins to hum an old Italian operetta. Without thinking, Gangi starts humming too, and after a while he asks, "Isn't this from Naughty Marietta?"

"Why yes, it is," she replies and they resume cooking and humming. When they're done, Gangi brings out the silver and flatware and he leads her to a table on the enclosed patio. Helen takes a seat while Gangi disappears inside to get juice and water. Once he returns, he tells her, "Let's dig in before it gets cold."

"I like your place here. How are your neighbors?"

"They're ok, I guess. Everybody smiles and waves. It's like they're on something," and they actually share a brief laugh. "I hear you're friends with that detective working the case on Elsie."

"Addie? Yes, she's fun to talk to and she's genuine. Get this, I think she likes me, we hit it off," she tells Gangi. "I like her, too," she adds sincerely. "It was really nice of Biggie to lend her his jet. She tells me he asked her to call him Gen. Only the best of his friends call him that."

Al raises a brow, "Yeah, and there aren't many of those around. Anyway, I don't think he likes where he lives. He thinks a lot of people are phonies, here or Chicago or anywhere, and he's sick of it. He's talked about moving here so we can be closer and visit more often. It's time. He's going to be seventy-seven soon. That's if a certain someone doesn't do a certain something and make a certain something happen."

Helen's not put off by what he says, it's what she came here to talk about. "You like it here Al? I do. The mountains are beautiful. I wake up every day with a clear mind, refreshed, looking forward to what I'm going to do that day. Sometimes I just go to a park or waterfall and just read, or hike and read."

"Yeah, I do like it here. We looked at a lot of places before deciding on the Smoky Mountains. The first visit we paid here I think Gen and I were already at home. It felt right."

"I'm thinking about retiring," she tells him wistfully. "I'm tired, and my time is come."

As they finish their meal, they clear the table and bring the flatware into the kitchen, leaving them to soak in the sink. Helen notices some other dishes, cleaned and sitting in the rack of the double sink. "You don't have a maid or housekeeper?" she asks.

Al shakes his head, "Too much trouble. I don't like strangers in my home. It's just me anyways. Unless I have a friend over."

"Addie told me about Daphne."

"Daphne, yeah. We're getting to be a thing. You think this place is big enough for two? I do. She spends enough time here, she might as well move in."

Helen pumps his arm with her fist, "You cad!" and the two of them continue talking like old friends. It's a little strange, but it's becoming easier with each passing moment.

Finally, Helen tells him, "Let's go back to the patio and talk about serious things for a moment. Why don't you call Gen and ask him to come here so we can meet? Get things out in the open."

Al makes the call and, hanging up, says, "He'll be here in one hour. That'll give us time to talk and take a short walk. I'll show you the area. It'd be a real trip if the three of us live here. Now that's how novels are made!" and they both laugh in agreement.

As they retake their seats on the patio, Helen tells Gangi, "I know Gen knows about the contract on himself and Elsie, or thinks he knows. You know, too."

"Yeah. It's kind of why I was a little worried when I saw you."

"And rightly so," she says, stretching out on the Adirondack chair she's in. "You wouldn't believe what screw-ups Spadaro and Mitch are. How they haven't killed themselves by now is a miracle."

"Their end is in sight," Al mutters, thinking out loud. "What do you think they wanted?"

"Revenge, I guess. Remember how Mitch got all those years ago when Elsie rejected him? Even I was afraid of him. He didn't act with any rationale, his respect for the Family and women were nonexistent. He was going to be put down."

Al agrees, "Yeah, his manners were very bad. And he left the Family to go to work for Spadaro. What the hell are you doing working for him anyway?" he asks Helen.

"He pays well and leaves me alone, the two best features an employer can have. Spadaro probably wanted to avenge his brother's killing. He knows he shouldn't have tried to grab territory in New York. He was at fault. But, he ignores the truth, and with this contract he's doing what he always does, striking out blindly."

Gangi gives what she says some deep thought, then he stands up. "Let's go for a walk, Helen. I'll take you on a tour," and she rises to her feet.

Gen has arrived and he knows that Al has ensured she's not a danger to them anymore. If anything, Al is thorough. He knows one wrong move means death. Still, Gen watches Helen to make sure and as he sits on the couch in the spacious living room next to her. Gangi is watching closely, his weapon at the ready. Gen looks at her, "Ok, Helen, tell me what's going on."

"I don't know where Addie got her information, but she's right. I met with Spadaro last May and was told to do a job on Elsie and yourself in July. I was called by Mitch to arrive in Asheville, and that the job should be done in a day or two and to get ready. I think I landed on the fifteenth or sixteenth of July and stayed near Mitch at an apartment they own. The call came on the eighteenth, from Mitch, and I paid your home a visit, but you were gone. Elsie was there, but she was already dead. I took pictures to prove to Mitch I had done the job and he paid me one million U.S., which is the first installment on the contract."

Continuing, "While I was in Heritage Hills, and near your home, I was passed by a woman on the street, and she waved and smiled. I've been enlisted by Addie to help find that woman, who is either the killer or maybe saw something to help with the case. By the way, Addie's a real nice person, isn't she?"

And Gen replies, genuinely, "Yes, she's a sweetheart. However, Skip tells me she was gonna stuff her bazooka up his butt." The three of them crack up a little.

"Did you find her like that? Did you find Elsie like that?" Helen asks, sadness giving each word a footprint.

"Yes," he tells her, remembering.

"I am so sorry," Helen tells him sorrowfully. "When I found her, my first thought was that no one, no one should die like that. Whoever did that is a monster."

The three of them pause; it's almost like they're saying a silent prayer, and maybe they are. Neither of them breaks the silence for a while.

Gen speaks first. His eyes are baleful, and Helen appreciates his emotional depth. "How much is left on your contract?"

"Nine million." The two men whistle a little.

Gen and Al look at each other. Gen's thinking that it could've been a hundred million, his reaction would have been the same.

"I'll pay the remainder of the contract," he tells her.

Helen nods and cautions him, "As a warning, Spadaro may have another countryman of mine to do the same job. I was threatened with a replacement." She pauses to let this sink in, then adds, "I'm leaving the country soon. You want me to do the job on Spadaro first?" she asks.

"No, leave him to me. I want to do it myself."

Then he gives her the marching orders she's been waiting for, "You do the job on Mitch, and this time make sure it's painful."

Staring into Gen's eyes, she answers,

"Gladly."

CHAPTER 14
INFORMATION

March

> I don't have a short temper, I just have a quick reaction to bullshit. Elizabeth Taylor

Gen opens his door, expecting Gangi. He heard him pull down the driveway, and he's happy to see him. Al had called earlier to tell him the news about the work-up on Reggi Thomas, that it's ready, sans medical history. Gen's pretty interested in this ever since he asked for it, and his interest is peaked after looking over her Facebook pages again. He muses, "People still use that? I could never get into it." After stepping from the door, he looks at Gangi's hands and there's a pretty big pile he's holding. "Wow, Al, that's a lot of material."

Gangi agrees, "She has a big family, and you said

to make it complete. I looked it through, it's all there. Roger's expensive, but on the ball. I like people that are thorough." He walks in, "Want I should spread this out on the kitchen table?" Seeing Gen nod, he begins to do just that. "By the way, there's some new construction near me, in Saluda. Why don't we take a look at it later today? Might suit you fine."

"Sure, sounds good. I have to get out of here. Too many memories. And, I think a lot of people know who I am now, or will know. I don't like people knowing my business," Gen says with a note of finality. After a short pause, he opens the floor for Gangi. "Ok, let's see what we have. Why don't you do the talking and I'll do the listening. I know a lot about her and her kids already, but I think it's always a good idea to know more. You know, we always want more," and Gangi breaks into a smile, nodding in agreement as he looks at the papers before him, deciding where to begin.

"Here we have a picture of her," he says as he points to an eight by ten.

"She *is* a good-looking woman," Gen declares, "she could pass for fifty."

"This one is Charlotte, her first daughter," Al tells him, pointing to another, "She and her husband Edwin have two daughters, Madison and Haley. This is them," he says, handing Gen more photos. "He's a retired ambulance chaser, and he made a lot of money at it, but they made some really bad gambles on stupid things and they've nearly lost it all. Millions of dollars. They live in Biltmore Forest, and they're members of the country club. I don't think they can hold on much longer. His money-making days are over since he retired from his practice, and she doesn't do anything. Her last job was in a tennis shop."

"Charlotte doesn't have an arrest record, but her husband does. It's for solicitation, and get this: 'Solicitation of a male prostitute, a *young* male prostitute, just seventeen.'"

Gen looks at the record sheet and sees the date. "It's probably what forced him to retire early."

Then, turning back to the photographs, Gen remarks, "Charlotte's cute, or at least used to be cute, she looks washed up. She looks like her mother. Girls are cute, too. Edwin's their natural father?"

Gangi sees the expression on Gen's face, traces of disbelief and doubt, and tells him, "Yeah. Hard to believe, right? Anyway, Reggi Thomas's youngest daughter is a politician. Her name is Megan. She lives in Raleigh. She's divorced for over ten years and has two sons, Patrick and Connor. Roger thinks she's either really bitchy or a dike. She's not remarried, not dating, and basically involved in campaigns or activism, getting in people's faces, stuff like that. Here's their photos with a workup of her bank accounts." He hands to Gen what Roger dug up, then adds, "She gets arrested a lot. She's like a professional protester."

While Gangi looks over Megan's bank records, he tells him, "Reggi Thomas's oldest is Francis Thomas. He's a private businessman, and he lives in Manhattan. His business involves the audit of financial records, tax planning, certifications of accounts, and ledgers. He's small potatoes. He got divorced last August, her name is Frédérica. You gotta see this photo," and he eagerly pulls out the one of Frank's ex.

Gen is entranced, "He married that? Damn. She's a knockout. He divorced that? What is he? A knucklehead?"

"Word has it that she was screwing everyone within striking distance and he had to," Gangi tells him with a note of brotherly understanding that men have for each other when things become hopeless.

"Francis and Frédérica have one son, Francis Jr." He hands the remaining photos over to Gen.

"Reggi Thomas's husband Joseph died a while ago, and that's it on the family."

"I know about Joseph. He developed Alzheimer's. Complications from it killed him," Gen says.

"Hmm," Gangi reflects, "Anyway, now Roger started to come in with some inside information from the stationhouse at 100 Asheville. Your detective friend Henson identified Reggi Thomas as being close to this very house—your house, Gen —on the day of the murder. Thomas says she saw someone else here, at the top of the driveway, standing there. Detective Henson has her looking through mugshots from the area to find that someone. They send the books to her house, 'cause she's old and it's the best way they have to engage Thomas, to help out."

"Roger dug through her email and Facebook stuff, and yes, she's telling people she's marrying Ken Jones. That Mr. Jones has a driver that lives in Asheville so he can go out and eat and drink to his satisfaction. The driver's name is Dennis Moray."

Gen is soaking this up, Al feels it. He's a good listener, always has been. There's been many a time in the past forty some odd years that Gangi has witnessed firsthand Gen's ruthless decisiveness. You don't want to be on the wrong end when he makes his conclusions and the fallout begins. Gangi wants to believe Gen is getting softer with age, but it's negligible, and there's no way in hell that the explosion that's coming isn't going to hurt some people.

"Ken Jones has a ranch in Wyoming. He has a caretaker living on site with his wife, and they serve as cooks and gal Fridays when he visits with his friends to go elk hunting. He stables horses there, and he bought Thomas a pony of her own, named it Princess. Reggi Thomas says, and I quote, 'it's beautiful when it snows, but it takes too long just to get back to civilization and go to the grocery store to get supplies' end quote."

Gen is listening, and he carries a look of concern and insightfulness, occasionally looking at Gangi, and then away when he works to grasp this new found knowledge, compartmentalizing it, storing it away.

"They bought a mansion in Naples, along with the furnishings. Here's a picture of it," Al says, handing Gen another photograph. "It's on billionaire's row, and they have a newly purchased eighty-foot yacht moored nearby. It's staffed by an engineer, a skipper, and a cook. The yacht is named 'The Flying Reggi' and they've taken some of his kids and their families out for short trips to the Caribbean on the yacht."

Gen is listening, he pays full attention, and Al continues, "Now for the bad parts. Ken Jones drinks too much. His drinking, insulting of wives, falling down, peeing himself, it's all gotten out of hand. One time he embarrassed Reggi Thomas with his drinking and she left him and flew home to Asheville. He chartered a plane and got to Asheville and met her at the gate. Thomas demanded he go to rehab, and he has, twice, and now he's finally sober. And I quote from her emails again 'There's not much else you can do in the middle of the ocean, except drink,' end quote.

Thomas managed his rehab treatment herself."

"They took a privileged cruise together on a pricey shipping line, stayed in the penthouse suite. Dined with the Captain each evening. Danced under the stars."

"Ken Jones's wife died from cancer, and it was a prolonged illness," Al tells Gen, "I'm reading here, he doesn't like hospitals. After his wife died, he simply couldn't stomach hospitals anymore."

"Ken Jones has a son in San Francisco, and he's an attorney and also married to an attorney. Jones has four other children scattered around in Denver and Asheville. One of them he doesn't speak to. His kids are all taken care of as far as money is concerned. Thomas speaks with one son who appreciates her effort in having him stop drinking. His name is Peter. One of the other kids thinks she's a gold digger."

Finally, Gangi stops reading and talking and when he looks up, he finds Gen is staring at him, "I'm done, that's the end of the report. So what do you think?"

After a long pause and deep thinking, Gen says, "I'm more interested in what Reggi's thinking."

After a while, it's apparent Gen needs some alone time and he asks Gangi to head out and grab some steaks. He wants to take a walk and think this through. They'll share a meal tonight and use the new grill that arrived a couple of days ago. It's on the deck, and even though it's late March, the weather is cooperating today. The birds are beginning to return from their migrations, making nests. The deck hosts a couple of tall gas heaters and maybe they'll have a drink or two while they discuss what all this means.

As Gangi makes his way out of the complex, he's driving slowly along well-manicured roads, with neighbors out walking their pets, waving and smiling. He waves back and smiles and impulsively wants to run them over, or at least he gave it a comical thought or two. Of course, he would never do that, right? "We're not in Chicago anymore," he says out loud. Waving and smiling, smiling and waving. People are way too polite around here, and he knows that they're the same everywhere with their jealousies and hatreds. Still, the South has an allure not found anywhere else, and the Smokey Mountains are its pinnacle. He'll tolerate the hellos and smiles to live here. Anyway, Daphne's here. His mind wanders to Gen; maybe this Reggi Thomas has what he needs. She definitely has a thing for Ken Jones. He guesses she doesn't know who he really is, which is good.

After he buys some choice ingredients for a man's dinner to be shared by two old friends, he's headed back and arrives at Gen's. While marinating the sirloins and making some garlic butter for the potatoes, Gen walks in, and he's got that look on his face. He's drawn a conclusion and made a decision or two and Al thinks, *I hope he doesn't want to kill anyone*, as he stares at Gen's expression. Slowly, Gen's eyes train themselves on Al and they're reading each other's minds, and they know it. Each strangely divine what the other is thinking, kind of, or at least they believe they can. It's a big reason why they stayed together all these years, and it blends with trust. Almost since the time they met in the sixties, when Al's dad Gianni introduced him to Gennarro, it's been that way. As they both grew older, each knew and felt they would work together and be friends forever, be loyal forever.

So Al's not surprised when Gen announces, "I'm not killing anyone...yet."

"Steaks are perfect, Gen," Al tells him after he stuffs another bite full in. It's a pretty big meal, with the steak taking most of each other's plates, but they spread out anyway and put their potatoes in its own saucer, loaded with sour cream and chives, bacon bits and butter nearby. Italian opera sonatas play in the background and the rich cherrywood table affords them the room they need to seat themselves comfortably with their full wine glasses. Things are calmer now, eating

always has that effect on men, and they continue
with their meal in silence with an occasional ob-
servation about the baseball season soon arriving,
or the boat Gangi wants to get before the weather
becomes warm so it arrives and is in the water,
ready for the season. Whether he's going to put it
in Lake Lure or Bowen Lake first. They talk about
fishing, but neither really has an interest in that.

After they finish and clear the table, they stop by
the liquor cabinet and grab the Woodford Reserve,
a couple of tumblers filled with ice, and cigars that
they stuff into their mouths as they head to the
deck. Gen turns the heaters on, and the boys relax
in the cool evening overlooking the downward
sloping property below them. The sky above is
filled with stars and a bright, white half moon.
A light breeze blows through the tall pine trees.
There's little movement out in the distance or
here on the deck as they contentedly pull on their
smokes and drinks alternately.

Gen speaks up, quietly, "I gave a lot of thought
to what Roger found. It's comprehensive, this full
work-up on Reggi. It lays a lot of problems out
there and complicates things with me. Her daughter Charlotte sounds like a piece of work. I mean,
Al, we've seen so many people self-destruct over
the years. What the hell is wrong with them?"

Gangi knows it's his turn to listen, but Gen will
need some advice, and he looks over at him in the
darkness, the lights from the living room shining

behind them. Gen will ask, and Al knows the counsel he'll give, but it can wait. At this stage in life, you don't want to make any mistakes at all. You need to be careful with what you do and how you do it. Careful with people you know and people you don't know.

"We know a lot more now, and I think I know what I want to do. I know you think, Al, that I go around laying suspicion on everyone, that I think everybody killed Elsie, that I'm wild with anger and frustration," and he pauses and bows his head. Then he tells Al, sadly, quietly, slowly, "I am. I do. I'm lost."

After a pause, Gen looks up and over to Al, "I think about her all the time. I remember our life together. She kept me from becoming consumed with our business. Kept me from becoming a shitty person." He pauses again, "She was a good cook, too," and they laugh together.

Al tells Gen darkly, "We made Riggoti good for it. That was a sanctioned hit."

"I know, but it's eating at me. The bottom line is someone did kill her. That's a fact. And now we know Reggi Thomas has information we want. I'll tell you this; if Reggi is involved, and I don't care if it's just as a witness, in Elsie's death, I'm going to take her close to death's door," Gen finishes angrily.

After a while, he's calmed down and he asks Al,

"What do you think?"

Al speaks clearly and slowly, "Patience. We see a lot of things play out all by themselves. We might find this to fall into our lap if we just watch it for a short time. Then we'll know what she knows. In the meantime, I'll ask Roger to check in with his source weekly at the stationhouse and keep us up to date. When Reggi Thomas spots who she believes was at the top of your driveway, then we'll know everything for sure."

At this, Gen releases a cloud of bluish smoke up into the black of night, takes a sip from his bourbon, looks over at Al and says,

"She better fuckin' hurry up."

CHAPTER 15
ADDIE AND
FRANK

April

> I know of no greater happiness than to be with you all the time, without interruption, without end. Franz Kafka

F rank looks out through his small window as the jet lands smoothly, wondering if this is going to turn out to be his new home one day, here in Asheville. He likes the mountains, and, even though he's lived in Manhattan most of his life, he's been kind of a nature buff. He likes the outdoors, and Asheville has plenty of that. He makes a mental note to look at a little real estate. He looks through his window again as the plane pulls up to the gate. It's bright and sunny this morning. The air is still and looks clean and crisp, like after a morning rain.

Then his mind turns to Adelaide. She's waiting for him, at the checkpoint, and he's hoping they'll pick up where they left off five weeks ago, as natural as two people can be with each other. That their conversation and the way they act with each other is easy and welcoming, and comfortable. Like they've known each other for a long time. But of course, they haven't, and he feels that's going to be the excitement they'll both be riding the undercurrent of. His seat on the aircraft is towards the front, and he disembarks quickly after the door has been opened, nodding to the pilots and attendants.

He has to stop himself from running. He feels like a foolish kid, excited to see his girlfriend. With an effort, he calms himself down, and, at that instant, he sees her, and she sees him, and he picks up his pace and runs through the checkpoint exit, picks her up in his arms and kisses her. Still holding her, she looks fondly at him, eyes clearly set on locking with his, smiling broadly, and tells him softly, "Hello, Frank, I missed you, a lot." As he puts her down, the security detail at the checkpoint are staring at them. Addie stares back and they hide their heads. They know who she is, and they watch her turn with him and leave. Frank and Addie are oblivious as they disappear into the terminal towards baggage claim, and the TSA staff begins to talk amongst themselves giddily.

"I'm not due back to the stationhouse for three days, Frank. We can do anything you want to do," she adds sexily, suggestively. Handing him the keys, their hands meet, they're warm, and she looks into his eyes, "You drive."

Taking the keys, Frank turns his head and swallows. He's finding it hard to think and he struggles to keep calm, "Sure, Adelaide," he tells her haltingly.

Once inside, they've both calmed down a little, and he turns the engine over and begins to drive away, "The doctors tell me I've completed my rehab, that I'm one hundred percent. I've got full movement in my shoulder, and the pins they put in can come out in four months, after the bones have fused."

Addie laughs a little, "You telling me this as a way of saying that I'm not going to break you?"

Frank is laughing with her, "I guess. You caught me! I guess I want you to know I'm ok and back to normal."

They pull into a space in front of her garden apartment and shut the engine down. As they both reach for their seatbelt release their hands meet again and freeze. Frank takes her hand in his and he strokes her soft skin with his thumb as he uses his other hand to brush aside her curls covering her eyes. He finds her looking at him, and her lips are slightly parted. He gives her a long, lingering kiss wet with passion. That's the only trigger needed, and they can't wait any longer. Each other's eyes predict the future plainly and they fight with the doors to get out of the car. Frank doesn't even take his travel bag, and they quicken their pace to her front door. The door is controlled by fingerprint, and it opens with a soft click. They're inside and breathing heavily, and they throw themselves at each other, trying to take each other's clothes off, buttons unfastened, clasps unhooked, and zippers being pulled. Frank hears a button pop and roll around on the floor, and Addie gives him her best casualty of war look.

He reaches for her again and they're almost fully unclothed. Their hands are all over each other, searching and touching, holding and stroking. When they break briefly, Addie runs for the bedroom and Frank gives her a head start to be fair. When he begins to charge after her, she releases a tiny screech as he grumbles lowly, reaching her just as she falls on the bed and they're in each other's arms. Their lips are on each other's, and his tongue is finding its way as she willingly allows him to dominate her for the moment.

She begins to stroke his penis, finding it very hard as Frank responds to her touch. His hand is at the top of her pubis. He's found her clitoris and he begins to titillate faster, then slower, then faster again. Over and over, they're enjoying each other's body and the pleasure they give to one another, trying to delay intercourse.

Unable to wait any longer, after they've been exploring each other's bodies, he rises to his knees and she parts her legs in expectation. He slowly, gently enters her and they begin the rhythm of lovers, as old as time itself. They find themselves laughing and groaning, moaning and thrusting ever harder. She's given up on trying to slow him down and is writhing below him, her hands clasped on the small of his back, stroking its length to his shoulder blades with her nails. Her legs are wrapped and locked behind him as his hands find her intimate places, and their lips are searching each other wildly.

Before he can reach his climax, she pulls him down and beside her on the bed and has soon mounted him, her knees next to his chest, his arms wrapped around her waist with one hand on each cheek, squeezing and releasing, her full breasts hanging before him. He begins to take them in his hands and massage them; her nipples are erect, and she is groaning louder and louder with each rise and fall.

Frank begins to laugh and smiles at how loud she's becoming. He tries to cover her mouth, but she pushes it away. He tells her in mock fear, "Adelaide! They're going to call the cops!"

She looks down, her smoky, glazed eyes are fixed

on him. She's nearing her climax and says loudly to him, huskily, "I *AM* THE COPS!"

Addie releases herself along with Frank's orgasm in two long groans in unison. She rests her head on his chest, and the two of them begin laughing crazily.

Over brunch, Addie's wearing her deep blue, terry-cloth robe, and Frank has his cotton pajama bottoms on. He's leaned in over his plate eating fried eggs, sopping up the yolk with his toast. Addie's seated with her legs crossed, scooping yogurt sprinkled with granola into her mouth. They're both famished and don't say much, listening to the birds outside the kitchen window, sunlight shining through. After a while, they're done, and it's very peaceful. The weather has turned warm in the past twenty-four hours, and they feel it's all just for them.

"I thought tomorrow you could give me a tennis lesson," she suggests. "I bought a Babolat for each of us. The tennis pro guessed your grip size, and Frannie confirmed it after sneaking a look in your closet, finding your rackets."

"Those rackets are pretty expensive. Can I pay for half?" Seeing her hurt face, he quickly blurts out, "Forget I said that. Please don't beat me!"

"You pay for the court time and charge me an honest fee for instruction, and I'll provide the equipment," she bargains.

After a pause, he innocently asks, "We still talking about tennis?"

As she slaps at his arm, she tells him she's going to take a shower. After she stands to leave the room, she stops at the door and looks back at him, "You coming?"

The shower is steaming the room, Addie likes it that way, and she disrobes and steps inside, letting the waterfall showerhead drench her. She tilts her head backward to let her hair wash away from her face, and that's how Frank finds her when he steps inside, arched, her head tilted, naked, beautiful, toned. She heard the door open and close and slowly brings herself forward to see him. She is instantly aroused. At fifty-four, he is a chiseled, muscular, handsome man. He looks pretty much like the picture she was inspecting at his mother's home that day last year. Only better, and, she thinks, naughtily, *probably because he's not wearing anything. Addie, you have hit the jackpot with this man.*

"I can read your thoughts," he teases. He caught her looking him over.

She's a little surprised; maybe he *can* read her thoughts. She soaps a sea sponge quickly and proffers it to him as she turns around, "Would you?" she asks.

He steps closer, and, with his hand on her hip, places the sponge on her shoulder, the warm shower falling all around them. He slides it down to the small of her back, then brings it back to her shoulder and repeats. And then one more time and he brings the soft sponge to her buttocks and begins to wash her. He reaches down and kisses her neck, and she closes her eyes and tilts her head to her right to let him in. Now the sponge has moved to her belly and it glides down and then up to her breast. His left hand has reached down and is finding her intimate place and he begins a circular motion with his middle finger, pressing firmly. Still kissing her neck, she begins to moan softly as she opens her mouth to receive some water. She's suddenly very thirsty. She can feel his erect penis behind her, and she reaches for it. They stroke each other softly, over and over. Slowly she turns to him. They stare into each other's eyes and she takes a seat on the tiled bench inside the steamy shower.

There is no way they will make it to the bedroom.

They've decided to take a nap and conceded to

each how tired they are. Dinner tonight will be downtown at this kitschy Japanese place, followed by craft cocktails in the local bar scenes. Frank and Addie are dressing in separate rooms. They agreed to do that after the morning, and then shower, episodes. If they're going to make it out, then they have to put clothes on. When Addie enters the living room, she sees Frank is already dressed, "Hello, handsome."

As he begins to move toward her, Addie opens her eyes wide and she cautions, "Observe the five-foot rule, Frank, don't come any closer."

Reminded of their agreement to not engage in touching, or anything, until later tonight, he holds his hands up guiltily, "Oops, you're right." Then, seeing the look on her face, he adds, "Let's go." Peering outside, he tells her, "ride's here." They leave, Frank first and then Addie, and she locks her door.

The next morning, Addie wakes up first, looks at her hand, and sees the ring on her finger that Frank had brought with him. Last night, he told her he wants to meet her parents, Irene and Jericho, and they talk about a trip to New Orleans, where her dad and mother live. He's a retired detective turned guest lecturer at various universities on criminology, and she's a social worker at Tulane

Medical Center. He's from Trinidad, and she's from Wisconsin.

After the date last night, they began to prepare for bed and Frank became amorous again. Addie put a kibosh to it, 'Stop big boy, you wore me out.' As they began to sleep she became aroused for absolutely no reason. Reaching over she heard him lightly snoring. And she stopped. She wore him out, too.

This morning, they're going to have breakfast together, maybe tennis later. It's modest, just fruit and coffee.

She tells him she might be promoted to captain if she can close this case. Frank lets her know he's been thinking about opening an office in Asheville and keep both offices. They talk about that night in the hospital. His pulse rate made the monitor sing. They laugh together intimately, sharing the looks that only two naughty people can share.

Addie likes blueberries and pineapple, and she picks up a few honey crisp apples for Frank. Frank looks at the apple, "That is huge!"

"That's how big they grow around here. But it's not growing season here yet, those are storage apples." After seeing Frank's reaction, she adds, "Almost all apples sold in supermarkets are storage apples, unless you live near orchards. They're perfectly fine."

Frank flips the apple onto his bicep and bounces it back into his hand and sits down to carve it up.

"Nice trick," Addie tells him. "Can I ask you something serious?"

He looks at her curiously, "Sure you can. You can ask me anything."

"It's about your mother." Frank is expectant. "Tell me about her past a little."

"Well, she met my stepfather Joseph over forty years ago. She got away from her first husband, John Paulson, because he was abusive and an alcoholic. He's dead. Both guys are deceased. Anyway, in her early years with my natural father, there was always trouble in the house. They fought a lot. When she met Joe, it was a blessing for her and for us."

"Anything you remember from those early years that sticks out?"

"Oh, plenty. But the worst time for us was when we, the kids, had to go stay with our uncle. Mom was in the hospital for around six months. We felt like she wouldn't come to get us. Charlotte cried a lot. Megan was just really angry most of the time. But she did come get us and we moved far away after that. I never saw my natural father again. I never saw his side of the family again. Later, I figured out we had gone into hiding to get away from him."

Addie lets this snippet find a home in her memory bank. Then she gets to her real intention for speaking about Frank's mom. "You told me she's engaged now to Ken Jones."

"Yes."

"Do you know who he is?"

"Yes. Edwin, my brother-in-law, told me."

"Do you know when his wife died and how she died?"

"Yes, last July ... she was murdered in their home in Heritage Hills."

"Then you know how this looks."

"Yes."

"Tell me."

Frank pauses, finding the right words. He's always been like this, cautionary. "Mom met Ken Jones, a retired mobster from Chicago, two months after his wife was murdered, and they started dating."

"Then I have one word for you, Frank."

Looking at her, he quietly says, "I know the word."

"What is it?"

He leans back, his eyes still on Addie, and says, "Collusion."

Addie nods her head, and Frank states clearly, "My mother is seventy-nine, Adelaide. I'm pretty sure she's not the murdering type."

Addie replies, "Well, something is going on, and I'm going to find out what that something is."

He pauses. Nothing more to add, Frank looks at Addie, then looks at his empty plate, then back to Addie, who he finds staring at him, and he says,

"That was a good apple."

CHAPTER 16
SPADARO

April 22nd

It's only a crime if you get caught. Russian
Proverb

T he black, angry tempest blows in from the
north over Lake Michigan, picking up
moisture as the arctic blast meets the
waters and reaches nighttime, weather-weary
Chicago. There, the warmer shores cause it to
stall, and, as it drains its low, heavy clouds,
lightning joins thunder over and over, coming
ever more quickly as the windswept downpour
drenches the city. Evil is on its way.

In the mansion on the hill sits its owner Anthony
Spadaro and former Consigliore Mitch Conti as the
fireplace blazes and shadows dance in the great
room. Lightning spotlights the old-world style of

the room, with library cases, books, and statues lining the walls. Grand style, ornate sofas and wing chairs rest on Persian rugs. It is in these chairs, before the fire, the two men sit discussing, arguing their next move.

"My advice, Anthony, is to reach out to Helen and tell her the job needs to be done in the next week," Mitch counsels. "And you have to tell her yourself, because she won't take it seriously unless it comes from the man who pays her bill."

"And my advice is to replace her. She's become stale maybe, too old and rusty for the job," he replies.

"If we get another resource for the job, then we get another headache. We'd have to take Helen out first, then Biggie. It compounds the whole picture. And what if the resource fails with Helen?" Suddenly a very close lightning crack deadens the great room, and the two men hunch and look towards the windows. "If the resource doesn't do the job, then she'll come right after us. She's good. You saw the pictures of Elsie, right? That was Helen. Imagine what she'd do to us."

"Mitch, it's a risk I'm willing to take. We have a lot of firepower to throw her way. You think I'm just going to sit around while she comes for us? Anyways, I decided, and we'll have a visitor in a while. We'll meet, agree, and then he'll do both jobs, Helen first."

Mitch stares at the fire, its warmth not reassuring him. "Anthony, how'd you get someone to do the job on Helen? They all stick together. Is your resource coming here to kill us?" He looks over at Spadaro.

Spadaro considers this reality, but answers, "He's not from around here. He's not from America. He's from Russia, and he's ex-KGB undercover. He doesn't follow the domestic rules of the hitman society," he tells Mitch sarcastically. "He was referred to me by a friend of friend of a friend." He lets this guttural, phlegmy laugh escape, the fire's flames accentuating his huge greasy face.

The housemaid is listening intently, and the house is still except for the activity on the second and third floors, where Spadaro's men and their goomahs are busy. The storm lingering overhead has everyone inside, taking shelter. If a passerby were to question her, she's simply performing her duties, waiting on her master for further orders. It hasn't happened in seven years, so very little risk is in play.

A black limousine pulls onto the property and stops in front of the huge home as showers from the storm pelt the windows and roof, lightning and thunder screaming out loudly, winds howling, wildly swaying trees and loose branches breaking and disappearing into the melee. Ulrich Pavlov peers out, disgusted, "Looks like Siberia, blech!" He leans back into his seat. It's warm, and outside is not. After a few minutes, he decides the skies aren't clearing and he presses the intercom. When it's answered, he tells the driver to open the doors and they will go. When the driver reaches his door, he's visibly struggling to control the umbrella. Ulrich dons his heavy coat over his head, holds the door open, steps out, and they make their way up the steps to the massive front doors where they open briefly to allow him and his driver to enter. The butler takes his wet coat, and Ulrich motions to the driver to bring his things in, "But maybe you should wait until the winds die down. I'm not in a rush."

Standing there, he hears laughter and music from upstairs, and an occasional shriek. Ulrich is shown down a passage to the great room where Spadaro is waiting with Mitch. As he enters, both men stand, and the three of them look each over briefly. Ulrich Pavlov is an ordinary looking sort, wearing a fitted business suit that reveals his muscular, fit stature. He wears round, antique horn-rimmed spectacles that convey his intelligent nature. His blackish gray hair is slicked back, his face gaunt, but well fed. He has a commanding presence as he steps forward to meet the two men, not sure of which is his employer, Anthony Spadaro.

Spadaro steps forward, his hand outstretched, and now Ulrich knows which is which. The two men shake hands as Spadaro greets him, "Thank you for coming, Ulrich Pavlov. Can I call you Ulrich?" he asks, referring to the more casual address.

"Of course, Anthony."

"Fine. This man," Spadaro says, pointing to Mitch, "is Mitch Conti. He worked with me for years as my legal counsel."

Ulrich addresses him, shaking hands. He can sense this Mitch Conti is frightened. He grins at him malevolently, releases his hand, and turns back to Anthony, "Beautiful day out, yes?"

The three men laugh a little, and the small talk follows, and, when it's reached its end, Ulrich asks, as is his right as the guest, "Tell me the specifics of this adventure we are all on."

"I think your English is very good, but stop me if you need to," Spadaro says. As he continues to tell him about the first job, on Helen, Ulrich develops a dislike for this large Italian, for no reason other than the man is pretentious, poorly educated, and slovenly. He definitely doesn't like either man, but he doesn't have to.

Ulrich understands the details of the first assassination. "Helen Richter? I know of her; her reputation is global. She is not an easily beaten woman. She is always on guard and armed. Is there any reason to believe this will not be so?"

Spadaro anticipated this and he tells Ulrich in his gravelly voice, "She is under our employ and she uses one of our apartments in Asheville, North

Carolina, sleeping in the solitary bedroom there. You will be given a key if you choose to do the job there. If you choose not to, that is up to you. We can't have her escape your attempt, though. If she were to find we are trying to eliminate her, it will be very dangerous for me, for Mitch, for you."

Ulrich thinks this over, "Her price will be ten million U.S." The two men glance at each other, and Ulrich adds, "Added risk, added reward. She won't escape me."

Anthony knows he's out of options. "Agreed. This is a recent picture of Helen," he says, handing him some photographs, "and we know she'll be in Asheville next week for two days, Monday and Tuesday."

And then Spadaro adds, "I want her left forefinger as proof of the killing, and as soon as it's done, we have another job, also in Asheville. You can stay put and do that one right after Helen."

As Ulrich waits for the details on the second job, he considers making a quick exit. He's not excited about taking out another hitman, especially Helen Richter.

Spadaro tells him about the second assassination. "The target is Biggie Battaglia." Ulrich lifts an eyebrow. "We want the job to be brutal and painful."

Ulrich considers this for a moment, "His price will be fifty million. He is a very dangerous person with an army of loyal men." The two men look at him in disbelief, and he then describes the tortured death he'll inflict. "I use a spearpoint in these cases. It is a strong, thick knife, and very sharp. Deboning is easy, and torture is a simple by-product. I'll record it for you," he ends, smiling.

Spadaro reluctantly agrees, and the housemaid is summoned to bring brandy, vodka, and port.

They drink to the success of the mission, make more small talk, and the housemaid appears again to lead Ulrich to his room in a more secluded, quiet part of the house.

He enters his bedroom, lightning rattling the windows, bright flashes of light; the storm is low.

He pours another drink, removes his clothes except his underwear, and reveals a heavily scarred body, with deep indentations where tissue has died.

A knock at the door is unexpected. He grabs a weapon and tells the intruder to open the door. It's a beautiful, little underage girl. She stares at his bare, tortured body and steps into the room.

He looks at her, thinks his options over, and tells her, "Please go."

After she closes the door, he mutters under his breath,

"My own daughter is that age. What is wrong with these people?"

CHAPTER 17
ADDIE AND
JUVIEUX

April 24th

Whatever you are, be a good one. Abraham Lincoln

rank finishes dressing, picks up his travel bag, and leaves the bedroom. It's lightly packed. He tucks it under his arm and enters the kitchen, finding Addie on the patio of her garden apartment. He comes close to her, kisses her, and looks into Addie's eyes, "See you in two days?"

"Yes, don't be long, ok? I'm off again beginning Thursday for a few days and we can spend some time looking at homes in the area if you want, and whatever else you want to do," she tells him suggestively.

He smiles agreeably and wonders if the novelty of his relationship with Adelaide will ever wear off. They've decided to halve their life, New York City and Asheville. Their careers are important to them; they've discussed it, agreed on it, and they want to make it work. What they haven't decided on is children. As an older couple, they find that topic touchier than others. Addie's not sure Frank wants another, even though he's told her he's not against it. And she's not sure she can even conceive. She'll turn forty-seven soon, and the threshold for her possible motherhood may have been crossed. But at least they've talked about it.

After he leaves to go see his mother—she's leasing another car, and Frank has offered to help her—Addie showers and dresses in full uniform. The windows are open, and a cool morning, mountain breeze glides into the bedroom, with birds busily crowding each other on the tree outside, chirping and flying away in groups as cars hustle by on the road below. Asheville is waking up, and it's time to start a new day.

Reaching her car, she finds it to be warmed by the morning sun, and, seating herself behind the wheel, checks her makeup. She's meeting with the commissioner again today. He wants to be brought up to date on the case of Elsie Battaglia. She has new information for him, but it can't be closed yet, as there are unsettling, open endings to explain. One of them is why Gen was so open about having loved his wife. The other is if Anthony Spadaro *is* responsible, then who is his instrument of death? Helen can't find it. And how does Reggi Thomas fit into this? She thinks to herself, *What the hell is going on?*

Her only real comfort is that the case is tightening, and she has a limited number of suspects, and someone will hang for it. She can make a case for either Spadaro or Gen, and it will mean life for each one, but she wants to be right. She hopes it's not Gen, but if facts lean in his direction, and it really looks that way, then she'll have to arrest him after presenting the case to the D.A. Why is life so difficult? And why do people do things like this? Is it always easier to just steal and kill? Cheat and lie? It makes her troubled to think of arresting Battaglia. She knows he's probably responsible for so many crimes and deserves it, but the comfort of knowing this, well, it's not there. In the end, she wants to be right.

Her thoughts turn to Reggi and Frank. She hopes his mother isn't involved. Even if she just knew about it, she would be charged also. Would Frank leave her? He might, and that would be devastating. She's already given herself to him. It would crush her, and her life would be ruined. She can't live, won't live, without a future with him. After the car crash, she realized how much she wants him and needs him to be safe. She told him he needs to be careful for her sake, and he thought that was cute, which infuriated her, but only for a while. If Reggi is involved, Addie resolves to *make* Frank understand. She is determined, and that's the Addie she knows.

Later, at the stationhouse, the meeting is over with the commissioner. Captain Leary asks her to follow him to his office so they can talk.

"You're nearing the end of your case, Addie. Let me tell you now that it's good detective work you've been doing, you've uncovered a lot," and he looks sideways at her as they both take their seats at his round conference table. "For some reason, people open up to you. Spadaro's housemaid. And then there's Helen Richter. I mean that is big. Even the guys here say hello to her when she comes in. You have a hitman helping you on this case. That is incredible," he ends, laughing incredulously.

"Former hitman," Addie tells him.

"Right, I stand corrected. And don't mind the commissioner, he's eager to have the case solved so her family in Chicago reduces the heat."

He looks at her inquisitively, "I don't see a ring."

She knows he's referring to her engagement ring, "I don't wear it at work. But yes, I'm engaged."

"Can I ask who the man is? No one seems to know."

"His name is Frank. He's a businessman from New York," she tells him evasively, but decides to come out with the pertinent details. "I met him while working this case. His mother is Reggi Thomas," she tells him, dropping this headline in his lap, waiting for his reaction.

Captain Leary almost falls out of his chair. "The Reggi Thomas of Ken Jones and Reggi Thomas?" he asks, his hand to his forehead. He's thinking quickly, calculating.

"The same. It wasn't planned," she explains. "If I tried to put him off, he'd have none of it. He's relentless, and I like it that way. We're marrying soon, and both of us feel the same way about each other. We've never felt like this with anyone else, and Battaglia or no Battaglia, it's going to happen," she flatly states, making her point that there is no backing down.

Leary studies her for a moment and decides there's no impropriety. He also decides to not tell the commissioner this, at least for a while. Changing the subject, "I'm retiring soon. You know that."

"Yes, everyone knows you want to begin a life of deep sea fishing and beachcombing with your wife and grandkids," she replies in a manner congratulating him.

"The commissioner has decided you will be the stationhouses' new captain, not common knowledge," Leary informs her, adding, "*When* this case is resolved. This is what I'm waiting for, and I'm not leaving until that is done. However, I am making my announcement today, and there's going to be some festivities at McAnn's after work," he tells her, and, reaching across, he puts his hand on her arm and conspiratorially whispers, "plan on taking car service home tonight."

Translation: There will be some drinking.

Addie Henson opens her eyes and finds she's in bed with her underwear on, sans bra. Her mouth tastes dry, as if it's been open for a while, and her head is pounding. The sheets are in disarray, and she smells like booze and fried food. She feels the other side of the bed, and Frank's not there, then she remembers he's gone to his mother's for two nights to help her get a new car. She feels her head because of the headache and fights back the urge to vomit as her fingers get stuck in her messy hair. She stops fighting and remains still, waiting for some energy to get turned on inside her so she can leave the bed and head to the bathroom. For now, she's reluctantly content to remain where last night left her. She needs some water, maybe a gallon.

Last night begins to creep back into her memory. Her immediate thoughts go to the arrival at

McAnn's. There must've been two hundred people there. She admits to herself that she doesn't remember much past ten o'clock, and dread overwhelms her. *Oh God, did I behave myself?* she thinks, *I'm going to be the new captain, did I screw that up?* First, she decides to spank herself later, after she feels better and the headache is gone. Second, she resolves to never drink hard liquor in public. Ever, ever, ever.

Then she hears it. At first, she thinks the clank of a dish is from outside and she looks up to her window and sees it's shut. She looks for her service weapon, but it's not on the nightstand, so she quietly, quietly reaches out for the drawer and slowly opens it. Feeling around carefully with her fingers, she finds the weapon, and, as she, quietly as ever, pulls it out of the drawer, a shape appears in her doorway. She freezes, and, as the shape nears her, light gives way to reveal the identity of the noisemaker. It's David Juvieux. In his hands he has two coffee cups.

"G'morning, Addie. If you feel like you look then you will need this," and he holds one cup out for her to take. He sees the look of total surprise on her face and asks jokingly, "You want the other one, too?"

Total surprise or not, nothing is going to stop her from taking that coffee. She drops the service weapon back in the drawer and, holding her sheet to her as best she can, takes the offered cup, sips it, and decides this is the best cup of morning coffee she has ever tasted. "It's strong," she tells him with hot breath, relieved that it *is* strong. She needs that. "Wait. Why are you here? What happened last night?"

David just shakes his head pitifully, smiles, and tells her to get up, wake up, and they'll talk. In the meantime, he's going to put something together for them to eat and kill the hangover they both have. And is it ok for him to go through her refrigerator? She nods helplessly and, as he turns to go, she asks, emphatically, "What do you have on?" She has a confused look on her face, head tilted to one side, mouth slightly agape, her hair a mess. Whatever it is he has on, it's way too small for him, and it looks like it's developing a rip.

"Oh, this little thing. Addie, that's your robe." She halfheartedly wants to smack him. He's actually laughing, but she doesn't have the strength. That's how he leaves the bedroom, trailing laughter behind him, wearing her deep blue house robe, and he disappears. But he didn't close the door. And the next picture of dread settles in as she imagines he must have slept here, with her, last night, and she wants to scream. She pulls the sheets close to her, slides out of bed, and stands up, unsteadily. She closes the door, finds new clothes in her dresser, and puts them on. Next, it's to the bathroom so she can do her business and clean up. She only put the coffee cup down to put something on, and she now carries it with her on the way to the toilet.

Her first reaction is that of surprise, as she doesn't look as bad as she feels, and she quickly cleans up and leaves the room to find Juvieux in the kitchen. She has a lot of questions, and, if David slept with her last night, it's going to be a really bad day for him, and for her. On her way there, she notices her sectional in the living room. Something is out of order, and the room is a little dark. As her eyes become clearer, she makes out a rumpled sheet and a throw on the sofa, and at one end, there's a pillow. Total relief brings her new energy and focus. She looks up to the ceiling, to the heavens, "Thank you, Lord."

As she enters the kitchen, Juvieux looks over in her direction, "Good morning, Addie, I set a spread for us. Hope you don't mind. I toasted a couple of English muffins I found. It should soak up some of last night's leftovers. Some party, huh?"

Henson, looking at the sliced fruit, hot coffee, and muffins, nods approvingly. "Thanks, David," then, rubbing her temples, she says, "I have a headache the size of Texas, and you are making it worse wearing that robe."

She takes her seat at the table, and, after he brings over a jar of raspberry preserves, he sits across from her. "We had a good time. Your captain's a nice guy. We're going to lose a good one."

She nods, beginning to dig in. After a while eating in silence, they both begin to feel better, "Leary has had an interesting career. He's respected. Did you know he's ex-green beret?" Juvieux shakes his head, and she tells him, "Yup, he came from a large family and left home at sixteen. Said there wasn't enough food to go around. He lied about his age and enlisted in the army. One day after returning from a ten-mile march with a fifty-pound pack on his back, he saw these guys in funny hats with shirts buttoned casually, joking with each other, and asked about them. He applied, got in, learned hand-to-hand combat, ordinances, survival, all that stuff. He served for eleven years, mostly as a military advisor in Cambodia after the Vietnam era."

Then she slyly asks, trying to pry information from him on last night's goings on so she can remember herself, "So you enjoyed last night? I didn't see much of you."

She catches him staring at her as he breaks into a smile of understanding, "Addie, you were with me the whole night."

"Oh shit, you caught me." Then, sheepishly, she adds, "I don't remember much after ten. Was I out of line?"

"Naw, you were way cool," and a second wave of relief spills over her. He adds, "We were both inebriated and your place was close. We took car service here, our own cars are still back by McAnn's. It took me like thirty minutes to make the sofa into my bed last night, I was so plowed. Anyway, last night, all you talked about was Frank, Frank, Frank. If it wasn't cute it would have been annoying." They both laugh, holding their heads.

After they stop, she looks at Juvieux, "Please take that robe off before my hangover returns."

They're waiting for car service to arrive so they can go fetch their cars. They know they're cops, and their cars won't get towed, but they don't want to anger the parking gods. This is the South, and polite manners lend themselves to following the rules.

David asks Addie, "So what do you think about your investigation into Elsie Battaglia's murder? Any leads? Talk is you are up for a big promotion if you can close this out. As soon as you do, I'll be taking action in connection with the surveillance of Battaglia's home, and that will mean a big jump for me, too." He's referring to Riggoti's murder, and that Battaglia is involved.

"I know I need to close this case, and I could make Gennarro Battaglia and, or, Reggi Thomas good for it, but something's wrong, and all the evidence I have is circumstantial," she tells him, adding, "I have another fellow gangster also good for it. So at least I've gotten down to these two final suspects and their motives. That's about all I can tell you."

Juvieux is confused, "Why Reggi Thomas? You mean the one with the dog? The one we found standing in front of his home in Heritage Hills? On the recording from July?"

"Yes, Battaglia and Thomas are engaged, and they started seeing each other openly almost right after the murder. It's got conspiracy to commit all over it."

Juvieux almost laughs out loud, "Where the hell did you hear that? They are so *not* engaged. They're not even seeing each other."

It's Addie's turn to be confused. Anything David tells her about Gennarro Battaglia is believable. Juvieux has had Jones tailed, and he knows every move that he has made for months, but it's possible the two love birds are very clandestine.

Addie then begins to tell Juvieux about their trips together; Florida, the cruise, his driver, and on and on. She tells him about the six-week gap when her son couldn't find her because she was jet setting with Ken Jones; at least, that's what Reggi's son-in-law Edwin said. She tells him she has seen Reggi Thomas wearing the huge engagement ring, it must have cost a quarter of a million.

Juvieux is looking at Addie with eyes that spell

bewilderment, confusion, apprehension, all at the same time. They look at each other. Who's right, who's wrong?

Then resolve enters the picture and he tells Addie, "Let's get our cars, go home, shower, and get dressed. Time to catch bad guys."

Looking out the window, he adds, "Car's here."

CHAPTER 18
REGGI AND KEN

April 24th

No man has a good enough memory to be a
successful liar. Abraham Lincoln

Frank arrives in Heritage Hills to help his mother lease a new car. She wants it to be a Hyundai, like the one she has now, and they plan to see Cassie at the Asheville dealership. She can afford this style of car, but needs help, a co-signer, in securing the lease, since her credit has been ruined with her bad spending habits. Frank doesn't mind. It's trivial, and if it makes her happy, then it's just one of those small stuff things that don't bother him. He pulls down her driveway and parks to the side since they'll be taking her car, turning it in today. Opening the front door, he calls out and hears her reply that she'll be just a minute.

He looks around at the neatly kept interior. It looks like a model home. If anything, his mom is a very neat, organized person. But everyone has their faults, and hers is money. She just can't save a nickel, and maybe being at the mercy of a monthly check from Social Security is what she needs. It takes her mind off of spending and diverts it to, well, better things. Like grandkids, church, family. He remembers speaking with her about Ken Jones and all the money he supposedly has. She told Frank that he knows her financial circumstances. Frank had asked if Ken knows how she became broke. After seeing her quizzical expression, he asked her if Mr. Jones knows what she can do to a man's fortune, meaning she would just spend it all if she could. Even a billion dollars. They both had a good laugh over that one.

Frank suspects Reggi is involved with Ken Jones and possibly has inside knowledge about the wife's murder in some peripheral manner because they started seeing each other in September, two months after his wife was killed. But the idea is farfetched. His mom can be angry and twisted at times, but she doesn't condone murder. Maybe Ken Jones does, though. He *is* a retired gangster, and his Family is not a smalltime operation. He did a little reading up on the DiCaprios. What he could get online reflected a well-run criminal empire, complete with well-paid legal resources, a host of legitimate businesses, and a comparably large host of illegal interests. It was not a stellar resume.

Then there's his drinking and binge episodes. If they do marry and he returns to alcohol, his mother will be back where she was with her first husband. He talked about it with his sister Megan and told her that Patrick, Megan's oldest son, would be the first to confront Ken Jones should he become physical with his grandmother. Things like that escalate, and the police get involved quickly. Megan brushed it aside, but Frank told her, pointedly, that crimes of passion happen exactly this way, and that she should be a little worried. In any case, he knows he can't stop his mother from marrying him. She makes her own decisions and always will. It's just a cause for worry, what with all this alcoholism, mob land stuff, senior citizens, murder, money, no money. And then there's Charlotte and Edwin, always in the background encouraging Reggi to follow through with her plans to marry Ken Jones. Charlotte has become money hungry and is willing to put her mother's, Frank's mother's, life on the line in order to prostitute herself and open the bank doors for those two losers. Frank just wants to go back to New York, with Adelaide, and change his phone number.

Elsewhere, while Frank and his mother head off to Asheville to lease a new car, Gennarro Battaglia, Gen, Biggie is rereading the report Roger gave them. He is on fire, and probably shouldn't have started drinking so early today. His anger is causing him to lose control, and that's not good, and he knows it.

He hates being alone in the house. At times he finds himself sending echoes through it, just to hear someone shout back. How desperate is that. There have been moments he wants to start throwing things—lamps, dishes, his glass filled with Woodford bourbon, you name it. He is angry, and he always sees satisfaction. He gets his way, and he's used to it. But not this time. Success has been elusive. By now, he's sure Riggoti didn't have Elsie killed and himself targeted. Helen made that clear. She was the button man, and Spadaro and that prick Mitch will eat a bullet and be humiliated and tortured at the same time. It's unusual to want to inflict pain in his line of work, but when it's personal, then it's personal, and slow, painful deaths provide a level of comfort, if you will.

Battaglia decides to confront Reggi today. He's fuming, rereading the report about her and himself as Ken Jones marrying is adding up to make him angrier and angrier. Who is she to be telling people these things? Battaglia is a very private man. And now that he knows Reggi Thomas is looking through mugshots to identify the killer, he is certain that she knows something. His patience is dying, and he wants answers. Only Reggi can give them to him, she has what he wants. If he has to threaten her, he will.

He decides to take a nap. He'll see Reggi Thomas later. He'll kill her if he has to.

Frank and his mother met with Cassie at the dealership and are driving away in a new Elantra. Reggi's pretty happy with it, it's just like the one she had to turn in. At her age, she doesn't want to learn all the new do-hickey's of another automobile. This one's black with a tan interior, and it has a lot of the features she likes—back up camera, heated and ventilated seats, hands-free dialing, navigation, and on and on. And it's cheap.

She looks over at Frank, "I told you Ken bought me a Mercedes AMG, Frank? I told him I wouldn't take it until after we're married. It's one of the reasons he respects me, that I live within my means and don't take his hand-outs."

Frank smiles and looks briefly at his mother and feels like barfing, "That's great, Mom." Inwardly thinking, *I hope this dumb guy Ken Jones knows what my mom is all about. He may be a retired gangster, but he's walking right into the lion's den. She will reduce him in size in one year or less. I guess she must be a pretty good catch, even at her age.*

Repeating himself, staring straight ahead while he drives her new car, "That's great, Mom." He looks at her again; she is so pleased with herself. It's comical.

"I told him he has to stop drinking and meet my family," she tells him. He's heard this before. "I said 'Ken, you are killing yourself.' And I think he finally listened. He stopped his drinking, *totally*."

"His family should be very pleased with you, Mom," he replies.

She glances at Frank, "Well, they are. But his son that lives in Arizona still thinks I'm a gold-digger. He's going to leave his entire fortune to me. He tells me his children are all taken care of. It would be nice to have some money, don't you think?"

"Sure, but you better get ready for a legal battle. Now, let's change the subject Mom. This is becoming morbid. Nobody's dying today. Tell me more about Ken, when am I going to meet him?"

Looking at the expressway, she tells him to take the next exit. She sees the expression on Frank's face. "Now listen to me," she says contritely, "we'll take the back roads home and skip having to go through town. Just take the exit, and then go right. No, I mean left. Yes, left, that's it. Just do it and stop being a baby."

"Tell you about Ken? Well he's seventy-seven."

"I thought you told me he's seventy-six."

"Well, he's seventy-six and a half."

"What? Is he like a little kid? When is the last time you told somebody you were so and so old, *'and a half.'*"

"Do you want to hear about Ken or not?"

"Sure, Mom, just giving you a hard time, go ahead."

"Well, he's a very kind man. I've changed him a lot. He's not rude with waiters and stuff like that anymore. He pays people better." Then, exasperatingly, she adds, "why is it that rich people are so cheap? He was paying the caretakers of his properties, his driver here, his skipper and engineer on the yacht...well, he was paying them the minimum. People can't live on that. I advised him and he agreed, and they're happier now that he respects them for their hard work, recognizing it with good, traditional pay. And bonuses, yes, that too. A lot of his clouded judgment came from drinking."

She adds, "Next, he's going to have to meet my family. I'm firm on that. I feel very strongly about having a close family. Turn right here, Frank," she says, pointing.

"What about Megan?"

"Megan and I are mending our differences. Things are getting better between us."

Frank is skeptical, "Oh, really? She's going to overlook the time you hired a private eye to dig up some dirt on her so you could become Patrick's guardian? That's pretty heavy stuff."

Thinking about the time when she and Joe didn't approve of Megan's parenting—it was really Reggi that didn't approve, Joe was just there to be her pit bull and yes man—she answers Frank, "We didn't really mean it."

"Sure, Mom. So when am I going to meet him? Do you have any pictures of him to show me?" he asks.

"You have to meet him before the wedding. I'll show some pictures to you when we get home. There's the entrance to Heritage Hills. You know your way from here."

They pull through the security gate, and Reggi suggests they take an alternate way home and gives him instructions on which turns to take as they drive slowly. People are on the golf course, in twos and fours, on the fairways, on the green putting, teeing off from the blues and whites, sometimes a ladies' group can be seen. It's a beautiful mountain day, with blue skies and tall white clouds. Pine trees line the manicured drive, and multi-million-dollar homes can be seen, set back from the road, nestled behind a sharp slope, or privacy landscaping and the like.

Reggi tells Frank to slow down at one point as they are crawling along, "That's Ken's place."

Below the road they're on, at the end of a long

driveway, sits a sprawling ranch in a valley that slopes away revealing the Smoky Mountains beyond it. It's a custom designed home, providing views and privacy at the same time. "What you don't see is that it's built into a hill, and it's four stories. He has an elevator in the house and an interior atrium in the middle. There's a palm tree in it."

"Why don't we stop in and say hello, Mom?" Frank would like to get an inside look into the lifestyle of the rich and famous.

"Oh, he's not home."

"Come on, Mom, how would you know that?"

"I saw him golfing on our way here."

"Why didn't you point him out to me?"

She looks at him, raises her shoulders, "Don't know. Guess I should have. Sorry."

Soon they pull into Reggi's driveway with the new car, the garage door opens after she presses the remote, and the car settles into its new home.

Later in the day, Frank is seated in the living room thinking about Ken's place. It makes his mother's home look like a cottage. The guy must be loaded.

Reggi floats into the room, refreshed after having taken a short nap. "Francis, you want a bite to eat?

Come into the kitchen and let's have a snack," and, being a dutiful son, he follows.

As she takes out some crostini rounds and pimento cheese, along with grapes and an apple from the fridge, Frank asks, "I need to talk about something with you, Mom. It's been bothering me."

She looks at him questioningly, "That sounds serious. Go ahead, you have the floor."

"You know about Ken's wife, right?"

She begins to place some crostini's in a small plate and fixing the other foods, "Oh, sure I do. Ken and I talk about her a lot, how it affected the kids. How it strained the relationship with Ken and the kids. You know his daughter in Asheville *still* won't talk to him?"

"No, I didn't know that. Anyway, you know what she died from?"

Reggi, shaking her head, says, "Poor lady. Yes, I know. Cancer. It was a long illness. Ken misses her. It's pretty bad. We pray together over it. I think it helps."

"She didn't have cancer, Mom."

"What? Yes, she did. Pancreatic cancer. That's what she had."

"No, Mom, if that's what he told you, he's lying."

At this, his mother becomes angry, and she turns

on him somewhat, pointing the fork she's holding at him, "Do not call Ken a liar. That is disrespectful. You take that back right now."

"It's not what she died from, Mother." He notices her getting fired up. He's seen this from her before, over his fifty-four years as her son. But, he's not backing down.

Now she's even more angry, and her face becomes twisted and she spits out, "Ok, honey-bunny. Why don't you just tell me what *you* think!"

Frank actually regrets getting into this, she's almost out of control. "Ok, I will. But you calm down first. We're just having a discussion, that is all."

Reggi thinks better of her behavior and she tells him through slightly gritted teeth, "Ok, I'm calm, go ahead."

"She was murdered in July of last year."

At this, Reggi puts both hands on the counter and stares at Frank with her mouth wide open, eyes wide open, a look of total disbelief. She stays like this for around five seconds, closes her mouth, throws her head back, and begins laughing hysterically. "Who the hell told you that cockamamie story? That is insane. Really, Frank. That is just plain nonsense."

Frank calmly tells her, "It's true. Want to hear something else? He's a retired mobster from Chicago. Ken Jones isn't even his real name."

"Oh, shit, Frank. Where did you hear that?"

"Edwin."

"Edwin? He's a bonehead. You know you can't believe anything he tells you, or Charlotte. They're the biggest liars on the planet. Really, Frank, I thought you knew better!"

Frank does feel kind of foolish. From the corner of his eye, he sees a movement, and, as his head turns, he spots a man, having parked his car at the top of the drive, is walking down the steep driveway towards the front door.

Reggi steps over to see what caught Frank's attention and she is completely surprised. A man, dressed in light khakis and polo shirt, leather woven loafers on his feet, eyes behind expensive sunwear.

It's Ken Jones.

"What's *he* doing here?" Reggi says out loud. Then, after catching what she just said, "He never comes over before calling." Frank looks at her, and she adds, "that's Ken Jones."

Thinking quickly, she tells Frank, "Why don't you answer the door while I go tidy up." She turns to go to her bedroom while Frank heads in the opposite direction towards the door.

Once inside her bedroom, she's wide-eyed over this visit from Ken, struggling a little to adjust her hair and apply some make-up. She can hear Frank opening the door and addressing the visitor. Reggi is as calm as she can be and waits a few moments before meeting them; she wants to hear what they're saying first.

Gen woke up from his nap refreshed, the effects of the alcohol long gone. After a shower and a shave, he looks into the mirror, evaluating the final product. "Nice job Gen, Ken, whatever your name is. Time to go see Reggi. She's going to tell me what I want to know or I'm going to slice her up." He turns away, opens his dresser drawer, pulls out his switchblade, and puts it into his pocket. He drives to Reggi Thomas's home, parks at the top, and walks down the driveway, and he is one angry man.

Before he can reach the door, it opens wide and a tall man steps out. "Hello, Mr. Jones. We finally meet!" The man has a broad smile, and his hand is outstretched.

His mind turning over, he decides, unhappily, that no one will be killed this afternoon. He knows what he has to do, and he readies himself, thinking, *this man is Frank Thomas, Reggi's son. He thinks*

I'm marrying his mother. This is the guy from New York. Play along, Gen. He takes Frank's hand and pumps it vigorously, "You must be Frank. I am really pleased to meet you."

Frank, thinking about earlier, says, "How was your golf game today?"

Ken answers, "I wasn't playing golf today. I don't understand," and he looks out of sorts at Frank.

"Maybe my mother made a mistake, no problem. Anyway, it's nice to finally meet you. I've heard a lot. You and Mom have been busy."

"Sure, I mean yes, we've been busy, what with a wedding coming up and all that. Your mother's a real catch. Sorry to hear about your stepfather."

"Come on in," Frank motions.

"I can't stay, I just wanted to tell your mother something, ask her something."

And at that, Reggi appears, and she's dressed in tight white pants and a flowery, flowing blouse. Ken sees her and whistles, then, "Wow, Reggi you look great," and he means it. She is a looker.

Reggi sees this is a defining moment and remains composed, and, as Ken steps forward to give her a brief hug, Frank steps aside. "Hi, Ken. What brings you here? Won't you come in," she says animatedly, smiling broadly that fake smile everyone wears around here.

"Can't stay, Reggi. There's a fundraiser at the club tonight and I thought you might want to know about it. I thought I'd tell you in person."

"That's really kind of you," she says, turning to glare at Frank.

"Ok, got to finish my rounds and let the others know. I'm off, bye." He quickly makes it back to his car before he whips out his switchblade and starts cutting.

Inside, Reggi insists Jones and she are in love and there is no truth to all that nonsense Frank was talking about.

Frank's head is swimming with what he just saw. He needs time to process it.

The next day, Frank wakes early, packs, and kisses his mother goodbye. Reggi knows he's eager to return to Adelaide.

CHAPTER 19
ULRICH

April 29th

> If you haven't cried, your eyes can't be beautiful. Sophia Loren

She takes her keys out of her handbag as she approaches the apartment door. Inserting the key into the lock, she then opens it. After she steps through the doorway, she pauses. Something is out of sorts, she can sense it, and she can smell it. She doesn't stop. Instead, she takes off her coat and throws it over the couch, places her bag on the dumbwaiter next to the door, and continues inside to the kitchen.

She flips on the kitchen light and walks over to the refrigerator. Opening it, she takes out a bottle of juice. Reaching into the cupboard, she finds a glass, fills it up, and, speaking out loud, tells the home entertainment unit to play some piano music. It's soon underway and she begins to head to the bedroom to put on her pajamas. As she approaches the door to her room, she hears a click. She stops and slowly turns around and finds a man behind her.

He speaks, "Hello, Helen."

He has a distinct Russian accent and, even in the dark hallway, she can make out his shape. As he comes closer, she finds him to be of average build with slicked back hair and round horn-rimmed glasses.

He tells her to turn around and put her hands behind her back. As she does, he begins to place handcuffs on her. He stops when he feels the distinct shape of a gun tucked into her waistline. He pulls it out and finds it to be holstered.

"I'll take this," he tells her in his thickly accented English, his hot breath resting on her neck, "it'll be my little souvenir."

Holding the barrel of his gun to the back of her head, he looks at her weapon and calmly asks her rhetorically, "Is this a silencer on your weapon, Helen?"

Helen replies patiently, "You can find out for yourself. What is it that you want?"

"You know what I'm here for," he answers her roughly.

"Then, I guess I won't be needing it anymore.

Enjoy it," she replies submissively, strangely.

After he cuffs her, he walks her to his car, not bothering to lock the apartment. She asks, "How did you get in?"

"Shut up, Helen."

As they drive away, she asks him merrily, "Are we going to take a hike today? I love hikes."

He looks over and says, "Shut up."

"Not the talkative type, I guess. If you're going to take me on a date, then you need to be a little friendlier," she tells him, almost singing the words.

She looks over at him again, "Ok, have it your way, but if it's a long drive, it'll give us time to speak to each other, you know, to share," and she smiles.

After a few minutes, he remarks, "You're not like your pictures, Helen."

"Oh, I'm not?" she asks coyly.

"No, you're a lot cuter in person."

She laughs a little, "Cuter? Maybe it's just the light."

"Too bad I have to bury you in a grave I dug," he laments sourly.

Helen just replies, "Oh, that's Ok."

The man gives her a peculiar look, thinking, *what is up with this crazy woman? I'm driving her to her final resting place and she's singing and telling me it's Ok.*

They find themselves on the Blue Ridge Parkway. It's deserted. No one else is on the road at this time of night. After a short time longer, he pulls off the road and takes a dirt path away from the main road.

Around a mile or two in, he stops the car, then turns off the engine. With his gun trained on her, he pulls open her door and tells her to exit the car. Using a flashlight to lead their way, they take a short walk into the brush on a little used trail. Before long they find themselves in front of a large, deep hole surrounded by rhododendron. He tells her to stand in front of it and turn around to look at him.

"Sorry I have to do this, it's just a job."

She replies nonchalantly, "No worries." He's staring at her again. She almost looks bored, and frankly, it's weirding him out.

He takes his weapon and puts it away. He then pulls her gun out and removes it from her holster. Smiling at her and looking the gun over approvingly, he tells her, "Nice pistol. This will be a great souvenir."

She's just standing there smiling, and it's really beginning to irritate him a little bit. He aims the gun from a safe distance. He doesn't want to bloody his clothes. When he pulls the trigger, he hears a click, and nothing happens.

He is surprised and suddenly, the feeling of dread appears. Helen begins to walk toward him, and he pulls the trigger again. Her hands are free, and fear overcomes him. When he begins to lunge for her, he finds out that he can't. Paralysis is beginning to grip him. He looks at the gun he's holding. He's been had.

"Drug-induced paralysis, on the handle you're holding. Goes right through the skin," she explains as she takes the flashlight he's holding.

He can't even look surprised, he can't move. She gives him a slight push backward and he lands with a heavy thud in the underbrush and dead leaves.

Helen, standing over him, inquires in a concerned fashion, "How do you feel? You look Ok. You're breathing, that's a good sign. I'm happy for you. Are you happy?" Not waiting for a response, she adds, "I don't think there's anything that Spadaro does that we don't know about. You were found the moment you stepped into his great room on that stormy evening last week that you're coming after me. I looked you up, Ulrich. Your habit of taking keepsakes made it just too easy for me."

Kneeling down, Helen takes the weapon from his hands, careful to use the barrel, leans over to him and whispers, "If you want to tell Spadaro, go ahead. He's a dead man soon."

Looking at him, "I'm going to watch you until you're able to stand and then you're on your own," and she kisses him on the lips.

"Go home, Ulrich, your daughter is waiting, you're all she has."

Mitch stopped off to grab some groceries. He returns to his car and begins to drive home. On the way there he turns on the radio, slips in a CD, and begins listening to some popular Italian songs. Soon after he begins to sing along, he feels something very cold on the back of his neck. The next thing he hears is a click and Helen saying, "Hello, Mitch."

He is instantly in total fear, and she tells him not to worry, to keep his eyes on the road. When they get to the turn that he should take to go home, she tells him to go straight. After a while, she asks him to take a right. The sign at the entrance reads "Dead End."

After a couple of miles, he asks nervously, "Hey, Helen what are you doing? It's me, Mitch."

She says, "Yeah, it's me, Helen. Listen, don't worry. We're just going to talk where we won't be disturbed. Stop the car at the end of the road. It's coming up."

After he does, she tells him to get out. She has her weapon trained on him, and they take a short walk and come to a stop at a tall pine tree.

She looks at Mitch and soothingly tells him, "Don't be so afraid. I'm just going to teach you some manners."

He doesn't know what she means, but he calms down a little. He doesn't believe she's going to hurt him any longer. She asks him to stand against the tree and place his hands behind him, around the trunk. He looks at her gun and does as he's told, and she cuffs them, strapping him to the tree. In the dark with the flashlight throwing deep, dark shadows on her face, to him she looks like the devil's right-hand man.

He begins to become afraid again. She looks at him, "Remain calm, silly. Nothing's going to happen."

Mitch meekly tells her, "I'm just wondering where this is going, that's all."

She shines the flashlight into his eyes, blinding him. When he begins to ask what she's doing, she suddenly reaches toward him with a long sharp knife and sticks it in his mouth. With one swift motion, she slices his tongue in two pieces.

He starts screaming, but it's not very loud. His tongue is gone, and his mouth is filled with blood. She slices his belly deeply. She looks at him and hisses, "The animals can smell this miles away, your stench. If they don't eat you, the insects will."

Looking at him calmly, she says, "Enjoy the nice, crisp evening air. Oh, and that stuff about not worrying and I'm not going to hurt you. I lied."

She walks away, gets into his car, and leaves.

Anthony Spadaro is really relieved that the weather has let up because he is sick and tired of winter. He's finished eating a nighttime snack in the kitchen, decides to head back upstairs and get some rest, maybe watch a few programs. It's a big day tomorrow.

The doorbell rings, his housemaid and butler have gone to their rooms, so he decides to answer the door himself. When he arrives there, he swings it open and finds that it's empty. No one is there. He steps out a few feet to find out if perhaps someone is going to another door of the house. As he begins to call out, he's hit in the back of the head and he collapses.

When he wakes, he finds that he's inside a small, dingy room lying on a little twin bed. Sitting at a table in front of him is Biggie Battaglia. And he doesn't look happy.

"Good evening, Anthony, I'm glad you could make

it. Why don't you take a seat? I know that mattress isn't very comfortable."

Anthony rises to his feet warily and, staring at Biggie, he takes the seat across from him at the table. They look suspiciously into each other's eyes.

"Take off your clothes," Biggie says.

Anthony stares at him, "What for?"

Biggie slaps him as hard as he can from a seated position and screams, "You know what for! Take your clothes off!" He intends to humiliate him before they go to the next level.

Anthony looks at Biggie disgustedly, "Go fuck yourself. I'm not doing that."

Biggie grins at him in a sinister fashion he's kind of perfected over the years, "You're going to do exactly what I tell you to do."

Biggie pulls out his gun, points it directly at Anthony's face, and Anthony's look tells Biggie that this pretentious stupid toad has never seen a barrel that big. When you have a gun pointed at you that close, that's exactly the way it looks.

Anthony begins to take all of his clothes off, and, when he reaches his underwear, Biggie stops him, "Leave those on."

Biggie reaches to the wall behind him and knocks a couple times. A door opens, revealing a room behind them, and a figure stands there, framed by the dark doorway.

It's a large man, and as he steps from the door towards them, Anthony sees a blinking machine in the middle of the room. It looks like an operating table with arms and lights blinking. Anthony is confused, and that's not good, and he knows it.

Michael looks at Anthony and says,

"That's Junior."

Gen steps into the room on the ground floor of the Glencoe Mansion and reflects. It's been a long road, and it's not over yet. Elsie's murderer is out there somewhere. When he finds that person, Spadaro's grisly death will pale. That person will be the definition of brutality, the wrong end. Each day is sad for Gen. What polar opposites he can be. One day he's a ruthless killer. The next day he's a sad widower.

As he's staring into space, the door opens and his nephew Vincent walks in. They embrace each other warmly, smiling, and when they break, they look at each other.

"How's retirement, Uncle Gen?"

"I'm still waiting for it to begin," Gen replies, laughing sadly, softly.

Vincent believes his uncle's been dwelling moodily. His eyes are wet. "It will end soon. Soon you will know."

"I have a feeling, Vincent, a premonition I will know very soon."

"Then the killing ends?" Vincent asks.

"Then the killing ends, yes," Gen replies, adding, "I know it's been hard on you. All these sanctioned hits. My behavior. The violence. I know it's not good for business."

"You're not a man we say no to. The Family supports you, even though it weakens us to make your case with the other Families here in Chicago. I'm glad that you'll know soon."

His nephew places his hand on Gen's shoulder, with the feelings men share for each other, and Gen drops his head a little,

"I miss her, Vincent."

CHAPTER 20
LOVE AND LIES

April 30th

It takes 20 years to build a reputation and five minutes to ruin it. Warren Buffett

Frank pulls up to 100 Asheville Court and hops out of his rental car. Reflecting on the past few days with Adelaide, he breaks into a smile. The two of them are becoming closer, and he can hardly believe it. Last night they shared a meal together and talked about their future. Addie knows that Frank doesn't want to leave New York City because of Frannie. And Frank knows that Adelaide doesn't want to leave Asheville because of her career. Regardless of their time constraints, they're making room for each other, and he doesn't see that coming to an end.

Each of them talked about their past a lot and

discussed experiences of prior relationships, especially the one with Frédérica. There are a lot of things that each one wants to avoid, like deceit, mistrust, the boredom of a stale relationship, and long spans of time without seeing each other.

They talked about children again. Frank remembers having raised Frannie and he told her of the commitment. A child can bring a lot of happiness into your home, and a child can also bring exhaustion into the same space. It changes a relationship. Instead of living for each other, the couple will live for the child first, each one of them becoming secondary. Adelaide tells Frank that she's given this a lot of thought and that she would like to try to have a child even this late in life. She wants it all.

Frank reaches the sergeant's desk after entering the building and asks to see Detective Henson. The man behind the desk gives Frank the once over, breaks into a smile, and then stretches his hand out, "I am Sergeant Maxwell, and I think your name is Frank, am I right?"

"Is everyone here a detective?" Frank says, laughing. "I can't get one by any of you guys."

The desk sergeant tells Frank, "It goes with the territory. Come on, I'll take you to Addie myself." He yells over his shoulder, "Hey, Lenny, watch the desk. I'll be back in a few minutes."

As they approach her desk, Addie looks up from

her paperwork and breaks into a smile. She's got the folder of the Elsie Battaglia case on her desk, and Frank's mother's picture is on top. The file is considerably larger than it was months ago, and Frank can see that there's a lot of material there. Still, no one has been arrested for her death. Addie stands up, and when Frank is deposited by the desk sergeant, she hugs him and says, "Thanks, Maxwell." Looking at Frank, she tells him, "Take a seat and let's talk for a minute."

Frank raises his eyebrows and, sitting, replies, "This must be serious. Sure, let's talk."

Frank begins first and he tells Abby, "I have been leaning in the direction that my mother is not in a relationship with Ken Jones, but now I'm not so sure. I'm thinking about what I saw recently, and it's making me think that everything she's telling me is true. I saw them together. And she knows so much about this guy."

Addie tells him as candidly as she can when she begins, "Agent Juvieux, from the FBI, has told me what he knows about Reggi and Ken. He's had Ken Jones, otherwise known as Gennarro Battaglia, under surveillance for months," she pauses to let this sink in and adds, "Frank, there is no relationship between your mother and Ken Jones. He hasn't even met her. He's a retired mobster. His wife's murder took place in July. And it's either at the hands of Ken Jones or another gangster from Chicago."

Frank is confused, "He hasn't even met her? Then let me tell you what I just saw. Not only does she know where he lives. She knows what his house looks like. She knows what the inside looks like. She knows there's an elevator in his house. She knows he has an atrium in the house. She knows the car he drives. She knows what he looks like. And he came to her house when I was there. I met him for the first time and when he saw my mother, the two of them acted like any couple *would* act. Hugging each other, making small talk with each other, smiling at each other, addressing each other by first name."

Before Addie can speak, and she does look perplexed, Frank tells her more, "My mother told me she began seeing him a couple months after his wife died, and she doesn't believe she was murdered, which is odd. They've taken trips to Wyoming, they've gone to Florida, and they've taken trips on his yacht. She's talked to his kids. He's been to rehab. He left rehab. He went back to rehab. They've been on junkets to San Francisco, Los Angeles, Washington DC, and New York City. They've taken a cruise together and stayed in the penthouse suite. They dined with the captain every night. Adelaide, you just can't make this stuff up."

Addie is really baffled.

Her case file is open on top of her desk, and Frank looks over at it, "Why do you have a picture of my mother?"

Addie replies that she was identified by an FBI agent as a person who was near Ken Jones's home on the day of the murder. "That's how we found your mom. She's going through pictures of people who live in the area and trying to find a person she saw that day."

Frank thinks out loud, "You say they're not in a relationship and I think differently. Maybe this Agent Juvieux doesn't know everything. Maybe Ken Jones isn't entirely truthful."

The two of them stare at one another for a moment, each one's confounded, and Addie states bluntly, "Someone is lying. Once we find out who's lying, we will know who the killer is."

Sergeant Maxwell returns and in tow is Helen Richter, and she doesn't look very happy.

"Helen, what's wrong?" Addie asks.

"Well, for one," Helen says, "I'm sick of looking at mugshots." Looking over at Frank, she asks, smiling slyly as best she can, "Is this your betrothed?"

Addie smiles back and replies, "Yes, this is Frank. Frank Thomas, meet Helen Richter."

Helen holds out her hand and Frank takes it. "Hello, you are the famous Helen Richter. Addie has told me a lot about you." Frank registers that he may have said the wrong thing. Quickly, he adds, "and it's all good."

Helen looks over at Addie and scolds her comically, "Are you telling stories out of school again?" The two of them share a little laugh.

Looking back at Frank, Helen tells him, "You are the one that stole her heart."

Frank adds, "It wasn't easy," looking askance at Addie.

Helen replies, placing her hand on his shoulder, patting it, "Nothing really good is ever easy."

Addie cuts in, "I'd like you to take a look at photos from Heritage Hills, of their members, we're running out of options."

Helen looks down at Addie's desk, spots the picture lying on top and answers, "Why? You already found her, the friendly woman," as they've come to call her. "Why didn't you reach out to me?"

Addie is puzzled again, "What?"

"That's her, how did you know? Just look at the chin, the nose, and the cheekbones."

"That's her."

Addie finds herself staring at the picture, and her thoughts turn to a multitude of detective things that detectives think.

"Anyway," Helen adds, "I just came by to tell you that I'm leaving the country. It's time for me to take a short break."

Addie laments, "I know. We've talked about it. I know you have to go. Is everything tidied up?" They give each other a conspiratorial look.

Then Helen tells her, "Yes, I gave my house plants to my neighbor and canceled my heat, I broke up with my boyfriend Ulrich, and I'm pretty sure he's halfway to Minsk by now." She breaks into a laugh. Translation: I didn't kill him and thank you for telling me about him.

Addie tells her that she and Frank were just discussing his mother and Ken Jones and that they are in the dark on this.

Addie adds, "Frank thinks they're in a relationship. And David Juvieux, the FBI agent, says no. At first glance one would think that the agent is correct because he watches Jones's every move, but Frank has very convincing arguments."

Helen mulls this over a while and comes to a decision, "Why don't you ask Ken Jones himself?"

Addie tells her, "That's exactly what I'm going to do now, good idea."

As she begins to punch in Gen's private cell, the man magically appears before her. He's with

Sergeant Maxwell, who tells her, "Detective, Mr. Battaglia is here to see you. FYI, it's getting crowded in here. Why don't you go to a conference room."

Addie looks at Battaglia, who carries a look of importance with some papers in his hands. She asks him if he's clairvoyant, because she was just beginning to call him. She has a question for him. Helen and Frank are silently taking this in, looking sideways at each other.

Addie hooks her fingers at the group and says, "Follow me." After a short walk they file into an interrogation room.

When they're all seated, Addie looks at Gen and says, "I talked to you and told you about Reggi Thomas and you didn't deny it."

Battaglia replies, "Addie, I am a patient and careful man. Experience has taught me to think and not react. When you told me about Reggi Thomas, the first thing I did was a background check on her to find out as much as I can."

Frank interjects, "You ran a background check on my mother?"

Gen takes a moment, looks at him, and says, "I thought I remembered you. We met last week, right?"

Frank tells him yes.

"You're Reggi Thomas's kid."

Frank tells him yes again.

Gen looks over to Addie and asks, "Why is he here?"

Addie replies, "This is Frank, he's my fiancé."

Battaglia is blown away. "This is Frank? Your fiancé? Frank Thomas. This is the Frank from New York?" and he puts it all together. "Oh, man. Why didn't I see this? You're Reggi Thomas's son," he says, looking at Frank, "and you're engaged to marry Addie."

Helen looks at Battaglia, "Small world, isn't it?"

After they've all calmed down from the revelations, Addie wants to ask Gen about Reggi Thomas, but before she can begin, Gen stops her. "The background check came back, and I have to tell you I have a pretty good picture about Reggi Thomas and her family. I also have to tell you that I am pretty ticked off. I really didn't get anything solid on the background check because it didn't include her medical history. The medical history takes a longer time to assemble because it's difficult to obtain and skirt the confidentiality issues, grease people's palms."

Addie says, "And?"

"Her medical history came in this morning so I stopped by to pick it up since I was in Chicago.

That's why I'm here. I just landed, and I wanted to come here and talk to you about what I found."

Continuing, "Do you want to hear something interesting? It says in the work-up of her medical history that during her first marriage, she was arrested. Apparently, they had a physical argument earlier that day. That night when her husband was sleeping, she attacked him, and the Memphis Police arrested her. I also found out why this was not included in her regular arrest records. According to her plea deal, she was placed under the care of a psychiatrist to help resolve her mental issues. She spent a little over six months in an institution. Her records were sealed. The arrest record should arrive tomorrow. I'll receive it by email."

Frank's eyes are wide; now he knows where his mother was those six months many, many years ago.

Addie can read Gen's thoughts, and they are very dark. And those thoughts are about Reggi Thomas.

She's also wondering what Gen was doing at Reggi Thomas's home. If he doesn't know her, why did he go there? Or does he know her?

Frank looks at Battaglia and asks, "Are you in a relationship with my mother or not?"

Battaglia looks at each member of the group there and settles his eyes on Frank, "Your mother's a beautiful woman. I enjoyed talking with her. You saw, you were there," he pauses and looks openly toward Frank, one man to another, bluntly telling him, "The first time I met her was last Thursday, the same day I met *you* for the first time."

Frank is thunderstruck. Addie let's all this sink in. Then she tells the group that she and Frank, with FBI Agent David Juvieux, need to go see Reggi Thomas to find out if she is involved in any way in the murder of Elsie Battaglia.

Addie begins to form an idea in her mind that Reggi Thomas is mentally ill.

She looks at Frank.

He wears the heavy face of a man much older.

She is sad.

She is worried.

She loves him.

CHAPTER
21 EDWIN

May Day
> The first thing we do, let's kill all the lawyers.
> - Shakespeare

Reggi had recounted to Charlotte and Edwin the luxurious trips with Ken; exclusive lodging, butler service, dining with dignitaries...it goes on forever. And then there's his vast holdings in real estate. It amounts to a small country! This man Ken Jones is super wealthy. How could Reggi have been so lucky? Maybe she deserves it after her husband Joseph's terrible illness and all the care she gave him over those two years. It must have been emotionally draining. The heavens have smiled on her mom—Charlotte is sure of it.

It doesn't bother them that they haven't met

Reggi's soon-to-be husband. They wake up every day hoping today will be the day Ken marries him. And the sooner the better, because what will happen if he dies before they're married? Then Charlotte and her husband lose everything. Her trophy wife days would be over. Her use for her older husband Edwin would become a thing of the past. They throw negative thoughts like that out of their minds and focus on planning for a bright, wealthy future.

Edwin and Charlotte are excited about today. Edwin's going to surprise his soon-to-be father-in-law and pay a visit to him. He wants to meet him, and Charlotte agreed that he should. He plans to ring his door at 9 am, and he hopes he'll be home and not playing golf or something. Since Edwin retired, he's had little to do except lose more than ninety percent of his fortune chasing unrealistic dreams. But he was bored. Now the prospect of being directly related to a billionaire like Ken Jones has filled him with hope and plans for the future. He almost can't believe his luck, and Charlotte has been giving him more attention than she has in years.

He presses his luck, "You look awfully warm and beautiful today, Charlotte."

She turns over in bed and tells him, knowing that he wants sex, "Thank you, Eddie. I think you'll like Ken, and I hope he likes you. It's pretty important you make a good impression. Will you take pictures?"

"Of course!" Charlotte looks into Edwin's eyes. He smells money. "This is going to be epic. I'll meet him and maybe grab a bite together, and we'll bond over lunch. You'll see, we'll be partners together. When I tell him about you and what a fox you are, I know he'll want to meet you too! ASAP."

Charlotte is oozing with self-worth, lapping up the compliment. She looks outside through the sheers that cover their master bedroom window, "Make sure you show him a pic of me? Make it a good one."

"They're all good, are you kidding me?"

"I think the storm clouds are beginning to gather. Later today we're having heavy rains, lightning, thunder," she advises.

He looks at her longingly, and she reaches inside his pajamas, finding his manhood. He breathes deeply and, despite her best attempt, very little reaction surfaces. "Maybe it's the anticipation of meeting Ken Jones." And she withdraws, leaves the bed, and heads to the bathroom to wash her hands of him.

Disappointed, Edwin does the same and tries not to meet her judgmental eyes. It's the first time in years that she's shown any interest in having anything that looks like sex. He just can't perform any longer. It's his age, his weight, his drinking, everything. Shit. He looks like a huge, darkly-skinned beach ball on two sticks, with wisps of silver curly hair barely noticeable at the top of his round face. It's over, and he knows it, and he resolves to salvage what little dignity he has by meeting Reggi's fiancé and inserting himself as Ken's new friend.

He thinks he'll take the Jaguar out to Ken's home. That's impressive. It's a twelve-cylinder, a vintage model. If anything, it's important to establish with Ken Jones that Edwin is a serious man, a man with means, and to garner his respect. They're not afar in age, and it's very possible they'll be the best of friends. Reggi asked him and Charlotte to arrive earlier than everyone else before her wedding ceremony—it's in a few months—to carry out some important family honor. They're both looking forward to that and especially excited about today. Sometimes the unknowns can bring even more enthusiasm to the front than anything else. Who knows what today will hold?

The future has never been brighter.

As Edwin takes the short drive to Heritage Hills, he's amusing himself, thinking about his first meeting with Ken Jones in his head. The Jaguar is quietly playing mood music as it grumbles along the interstate. Occasionally, a light rain passes overhead, foretelling of the storm that is just over the western horizon. It's supposed to be a big one, and Edwin wants to meet Ken while it's still dry out. Then it's back to the warm safety of home before the thunderheads arrive. As he comes nearer and nearer to Heritage Hills, he feels his stomach twisting in anticipation of meeting this legendary man, Ken Jones, and Edwin's hoping to live up to his expectations. He doesn't want to disappoint.

Battaglia opens the email he received from Roger this morning. It has an attachment labeled: DIA-VirginiaEileenPaulson19760514. He pauses for a moment to read the message from Roger. He's telling Gen that he has only sent this to him. It's sensitive stuff, and if Gen forwards it to Gangi, then to please make sure it doesn't get any further. He doesn't want it traced back to himself, in Chicago. He had to really dig to get it, and his sources would be blown if it comes back to him. Gen understands and replies with his assurances that it won't go further, Gen's eyes only. He signs the reply as Gennarro B, and off it goes.

Then he opens the attachment. It's a dismissal in case of adjournment, a DIA, concerning Virginia Paulson, from Reggi's first marriage. Once the individual completes his or her treatment, or complies with the plea's terms, the case is sealed, and the record is expunged of the offense. As he opens the attachment, he finds it to be lengthy and wordy. It takes a while to find the arresting officers' testaments and when he does, his eyes pay full attention. He rereads the two pages four or five times. When he stops reading the testaments, he finishes the entire document quickly, finding nothing else of value, and he returns to the testaments and reads them again. When he's done, he hangs his head, turning away from the monitor, and he begins to cry. Quietly at first, then it turns to be uncontrollable. His chest is heaving between gasps for air and he slams his fist down onto the table. Over and over, until he's spent, and a determined rage fills him. He suddenly has become very dangerous, this Gennarro Battaglia. He assumes his embodiment of a controlled, focused, instrument of death that he uses when purpose is before him.

Gen looks at his cell and picks it up. He needs to call Gangi and, as he does so, the doorbell rings. Gen's in a room deep inside the rear of the house. He stands and puts his switchblade into his trousers. Some habits die hard. He leaves the room, the attachment from Roger still visible on the monitor.

Instead of taking the trip to look at the video feed from the front door camera, he decides to answer it. Whoever it is will be asked to return later or simply turned away. He stops to look at himself in the mirror of the nearest bathroom, brushes back his hair, and blows his nose, then continues on to the door and opens it. His first thoughts are surprise and his second thoughts are about fate. Fate has dropped this into his lap, this visitor, and he quickly decides exactly what he'll do.

"Hello, are you Edwin?" he asks, smiling that fake smile. He remembers the pictures of Edwin and Charlotte from the original work-up that Roger did. Let's face it, not too many people look like Edwin. And as he recalls the photograph of him and Charlotte together, Gen couldn't help thinking that they made a very odd couple. He even finds Edwin indelibly printed in his mind. Very strange-looking man.

"I am well! Thank you!" Edwin tells him enthusiastically while holding out his hand, "I am really pleased to meet you, Ken!"

Ken looks at the proffered hand and lightly slaps it aside, "That won't do. We're going to be family soon!" Ken steps forward to embrace Edwin, who is plainly more than pleased at Ken's warmth and inviting hug, thinking, *this is already going well*, and Edwin finds himself immensely satisfied over his plan to come here and meet Ken Jones.

Ken, looking at the skies, tells Edwin, "Bring your car into the garage. That way, when you leave, you won't get wet. Don't worry, it's a big garage. It has a lot of space."

After the car is put away and the garage door closes, Ken beckons him, "Come in, Edwin. Let's talk awhile." Ken motions for Edwin to follow him. Looking over his shoulder, he remarks, "I'm assuming you're here as a follow-up to my having met your brother-in-law last week."

At that, Edwin is a little disappointed that Frank didn't tell him about meeting Ken Jones. It kind of takes the novelty out of meeting him now, not being the first to see him, but it doesn't deter him. He'll be the bigger person and see it through, thinking, *my character is stronger than that. Ken will see me for who I am.*

As they walk to the living room and sit down next to each other on the long couch, Ken is thinking and looking Edwin over, *this prick believes I'm his cash cow. He's here to ingratiate himself as my buddy. Reggi's convinced her entire family I'm marrying her, and then Edwin here will have access to my fortune. It'll be exactly what he needs to get out of debt. He's desperate.* Ken smiles at Edwin, who smiles back.

"Nasty storm coming today," Edwin comments.

He wants to talk about the weather, what an idiot, Jones mulls, then tells him, "Not to worry, Edwin, you're safe here. My house is your house." Ken can tell Edwin's about to cream his jeans.
"Mind if I call you Ed?" he asks.

"Not at all, my close friends call me Ed or Eddie, and you can too," he eagerly tells Ken.

"Can I show you around? This home is really something. I designed it myself," which is a lie, and they both stand. With Ken leading the way, they make it to the atrium that's in the middle of the house. Edwin whistles, seeing that it's three floors tall, with a palm tree in the middle that's seated on a small, sandy island at the bottom, on the first floor below, dotted with smaller trees. Looking outwards beyond the palm tree, Edwin sees the hilltops of the Smoky Mountains and is embarrassingly envious of Ken Jones's wealth. The view is unparalleled, it's sweeping. This isn't a home, it's a mansion. From the front it appears to be a simple, sprawling ranch. From the inside, it's four floors of opulence. This had to cost over one hundred million to build. It's more money than Edwin ever dreamed of having access to.

Ken lets this little shit take all of it in, thinking, *if I could read minds I'd say Ed here is putting a dollar figure on this house and he is deeply impressed. He's also thinking what he'll do once he has access to all that money. I don't even have to be a mind reader. His thoughts are clearly obvious. Wow.*

Ken tells Ed, "You like? C'mon, I'll take you down to the bottom, then we'll take the elevator up."

"You have an elevator?" Edwin is almost tongue-tied, and he follows Ken.

When they're done, they arrive back on the top floor and head to the living room again. When each has taken a seat on the couch, like before,

Edwin remarks, "This is a beautiful home, Ken. Can I ask you a question?"

"Sure, Ed, ask away." He wants to see how far Ed will go and decides to really creep him out. Ken's going to enjoy this.

"Is this where they found your wife?" Ed asks, pointing to the rug in front of them.

Ken looks at Ed, and Ken's fake smile has left his face. Edwin stares back, somewhat unsure of what will come next. After a brief pause, Ken places his hand high up on Ed's thigh, and, squeezing it, he asks, "Who's 'they'?"

Edwin is taken off guard. While staring at Ken's hand, he stammers, "Sorry, I didn't mean to offend?"

Ken removes his hand slowly, gently stroking Edwin's thigh as he pulls it away. Ken assumes the smile again, and Edwin is put at ease, for now. "Hey Ed, want to do a few lines of cocaine?"

Edwin doesn't know what to say. He didn't expect to hear that from Ken in a million years, and he replies meekly, "It's a little too early, don't you think?" Inwardly, he's worried that snorting cocaine might be fun, but he doesn't want to have a heart attack.

"Aw, c'mon, Eddie." Jones leans over to the end table, opens the drawer, and removes a silver box. Flipping open the lid, he pulls out a bag of white powder, a short silver straw, a mirror, and a razor blade. He begins to pour out some coke onto the mirror and forms two heavy lines around a couple of inches long. He spies from the corner of his eye that Edwin is watching him and he doesn't know what to say or how to get out of this. Handing Ed the straw, Ken smiles and says, "You first, you're my guest."

Ed takes the silver straw and, seeing no recourse, leans over to put the dust up his nose. It's a pretty heavy line, and when he finishes, he sneezes loudly. Ken laughs and snorts his line also and there they are, two men bonding over cocaine as future in-laws.

Their conversation eventually turns to family as Ken tells Ed, "Reggi is a fine woman, I'm fortunate to have met her. Can I tell you a secret, Ed?"

Ed nods, and Ken draws out more lines. "The sex with Reggi is out of this world. She does *everything*," Ken tells him, leering naughtily, noticing Edwin's response. "You ever had sex with your mother-in-law, Ed?"

Ed gives Ken a strange look. "I don't think like that, Ken. It never crossed my mind," and he shudders a little.

"Well, you should give it your consideration, my man. She is wild. She's also told me she fantasizes about you a lot." He places his hand on Edwin's thigh again and begins to rub it. "I'm thinking about joining a private men's club in Asheville. Some of the guys call it the Little Boys Club. You heard of it, Ed?"

Edwin's face registers shock, that's *his* boys club.

Ken knows Ed's a member there and he decides to turn it up a notch. While his hand is still on Edwin's thigh, he tells him, "I feel like having sex." He's looking directly into Edwin's eyes. Ken reads his thoughts and knows Edwin is totally freaked out. But, before Edwin can turn and run out of there, he tells him, "You know, if you have the money, you can get anything, any time of day." He takes his hand off Edwin's thigh, picks up his cell, and dials a number. When it's answered, Ken stands up and takes a few steps away. Speaking quietly into the phone so Edwin can't hear, he places his order and then he returns to the couch.

Ken decides to let up on Edwin a little. The best is yet to come. They return to making small talk and do a few more lines. After some time passes, the doorbell rings and Edwin has the look of surprise and guilt at the same time. He wasn't expecting a visitor, and doesn't want anyone to find them doing drugs.

Ken reassures Edwin, smiling sadistically, "The girls are here." He stands up to answer the door. When he opens it, he finds a petite blonde with a beautiful figure and a bookshelf rear-end. Beside her is a taller girl, also beautiful, a transvestite. As he escorts them in, he quietly gives them instructions. Walking into the living room, the girls are giggling, and he tells Edwin, "The taller one says she wants *you*."

They disappear into the dark recesses of the house, taking the cocaine with them. Ken orders the entertainment system to play some loud rock, and the party is underway.

When they emerge over an hour later, the girls leave, and Edwin discovers it's a little after 11 am in the morning. He feels like he's been up for days.

Seated at the breakfast bar, Ken is slicing up apples and oranges for them to share. "Gotta keep our energy levels up. That was like an exercise class." They're both laughing loudly. "C'mon, let's sit at the table over there and have some juice, share this fruit. If we need it, I'll get more."

After they've taken seats, Edwin tells him, as if possessing inside knowledge, "I know who you are."

"Oh really," Ken replies.

"Yes, I looked you up."

"And?"

"You trafficked in stolen goods. You were involved in sex slavery. You were involved in insurance fraud. Bribery and forgery, drugs. You're worth a lot of money."

"How much?"

"At least a billion."

"Wow," Ken reacts, playing along. "Did you know I put a man into a commercial woodchipper? Alive?"

Edwin doesn't say anything. He's beginning to get creeped out again. Ken can see he's afraid. You can't hide that forever.

Ken stares into Edwin's eyes and gets a little closer to him, almost whispering, "Did you know I skinned a man? That's a real thing. There's a technique to it, to remove their skin, in one piece, while they're still alive." Ken laughs a little, under his breath. "He screamed like there was no tomorrow. And guess what? There wasn't!" He laughs out loud, throwing his head back. Looking into Edwin's eyes again, he whispers, grinning, "Another guy, we took him apart piece by piece. That was a *trip*!"

Edwin dares to ask, skeptically, "But you're retired now, right?"

"Am I, Eddie?"

"You're marrying my mother-in-law, right?"

"Am I?" Ken knows the conversation has taken a turn into hell. "I'll let you in on some things, Edwin. I don't even know Reggi. I met her last week for the first time. I know she's been telling people we're engaged, that we take trips together, that we own a yacht." Edwin's eyes are large white pools of fear. Then Ken adds maliciously, through clenched teeth, "All lies."

He lets that revelation take charge. Holding up his cell phone, Ken asks, "You like pictures, Edwin? I have some right here. I just got them from your he-she you were getting banged by." He shows Edwin a few shots, a little oral here, a little rough riding there. "Reggi and Charlotte will love these. Your daughters, too," he says, smiling. "They're going viral, I'll see to that." He grins viciously at Edwin, his lips curled.

Edwin is deathly afraid. "You wouldn't do that, would you?" He begins to cry. He puts his hands to his head and then rests them on the table while sobbing softly.

In one swift motion, Ken brings the knife he was using to core the apple down into the meat of Edwin's hand, pinning it to the table with a loud bang. Edwin screams in pain. From his pocket Ken draws his switchblade and pops it open. Holding Edwin's arm still with his left hand, he skins it from elbow to wrist, deftly, as Edwin continues screaming. Then he reaches down, stabbing him in the crotch, and blood instantly appears in a widening pool at Edwin's feet. Quickly, Ken stands up and steps behind Edwin, holding his head still as he slices open one eye.

Trying to get away, Edwin rips his hand from the

knife, and, before he can take a step, Ken throws him to the floor, onto Edwin's huge belly. Ken takes the switchblade and inserts it deeply into his anus, twisting it, and he rests his knee on Edwin's back, holding him there as his screams reach a higher octave. Grabbing one hand, he removes all of Edwin's fingers, leaving the thumb, and quickly does the same to the other hand. From his position, and with Edwin screaming and squirming below him, Ken shouts, "And now I will treat you to a show! I'll skin *you* alive, just like that other lucky fellow!" With that, he runs his blade from shoulder to shoulder, around an inch deep. Then he runs it down each arm to the elbow and finishes the job, leaving Edwin screaming in a higher octave than ever.

Soon, Edwin is no longer moving, or breathing. Ken, still quite coked up, heads to the bath off the living room and cleans himself at the sink. After changing his clothes, he puts the bloody ones into the trash and calls Gangi to help him dispose of the body. When Gangi arrives, he sees Edwin lying in a pool of blood with torn skin. He knows what Gennarro Battaglia can do. "Got you pretty pissed, did he?"

Gen nods, and the two of them take him to Edwin's car in the garage. They tie him to the passenger seat and ram a long garden stake down his throat to hold his head up, and then they put Gangi's hat on him, covering his eyes. Gangi gets into the driver's seat and puts on Edwin's hat that's lying in the back seat. With the darkly tinted Jaguar windows, the agents watching the house won't know what's what. They'll just observe casually two men, Edwin and Gangi, pulling away in Edwin's car. As the garage door opens, Gen gets into his own car, and they drive away together.

After they've deposited Edwin's car and body for disposal later, Gen and Gangi return in Gen's car, and he and Gangi part ways.

Gen calmly walks into the house and sits down at the breakfast bar. He looks at his watch; it's one o'clock. In the time span of four hours, Edwin arrived, did coke, had sex, got sliced up, skinned, then was prepared to be dumped in Lake Lure. *I am impressed with myself*, he thinks, *that's a record*.

Glancing over at the blood, he doesn't think Elsie would have approved of him killing Edwin. Staring at the mess again, he remarks,

"I hope Addie doesn't find out about this."

CHAPTER 22 REGGI

May Day

> I'm not upset that you lied to me, I'm upset that from now on I can't believe you. Friedrich Nietzsche

I t's after lunch as Frank pulls up to the stationhouse inside Asheville. He leaves the rental car in the parking lot and walks in to find Adelaide standing with a man discussing something intently. As he approaches, she looks at him seriously, and she introduces Agent David Juvieux. The two men shake hands and make small talk, getting to know each other.

Frank remarks, "I heard the captain's retirement party was a real blast."

Addie and David look at each other guiltily. Frank knows he put them on the spot. "I heard there was a little sleepover. That's out there. I get it. Sometimes you need a release and end up with too much to drink. By the way, how was the couch? Comfy?"

Juvieux remarks, "So you're the Frank that Addie's always talking about. The night of the party everything was Frank, Frank, Frank," he adds, imitating her.

Addie rolls her eyes, then tells the two of them, "That's enough, guys, we have a lot to do today. Frank, we're going to go see your mother. We want to find out what's going on. I don't have to tell you that I think your mother has had a recurrence of her issues from years ago. We don't know how far this has gone, but it's definitely bizarre."

Frank then replies, "I've seen her acting things out when she came for a visit recently. I asked her what she was up to and she brushed it off. I let it go. Maybe I shouldn't have done that."

Addie tells him, "Don't blame yourself. Let's just head out there and talk to your mother. Did you call her?"

Frank answers, "Yes, I told her I was coming. She'll be a little surprised when she sees the two of you."

"It has to be done," Addie says. "I'm bringing David because he knows more about the area and the goings-on around the house where Jones lives."

Juvieux adds, "It's going to be just me, and I'm not bringing any of my other agents. We don't want to spook your mother."

As they begin to walk outside, they see thunder clouds approaching. The group can hear rumblings in the distant west.

Frank looks up to the sky. "It looks like it's going to be a really wet day. Let's see if we can get this done before the rains arrive."

They all climb into Addie's car and head off towards Heritage Hills. As they drive along, each of them is quietly thinking things over. What they'll say. What they'll see. What kind of reaction they'll get.

Addie looks at and thinks about Frank. *This is his mother. Reggi's not going to be happy to see her future daughter-in-law. She might never want to see me again. But things are beginning to add up, and, once again, reality bites. Frank doesn't know everything I plan to ask Reggi. If she gives me the answer I expect, then we'll know who killed Elsie Battaglia.*

Frank is concerned for Adelaide. He knows what she has to do. It's going to be unpleasant for her. He's going to be there to witness it, and he knows he's not looking forward to a very nice day. Inside, his mind is like the storm above. It's almost out of control.

David feels like a third wheel, but this will impact his case and his career. This concerns Jones, and anything that concerns Jones concerns Juvieux. Once Addie is done with her case, then he'll arrest Battaglia for the murder of Joseph Riggoti. Then they'll pick up Alberto Gangi. The other suspect, Michael Seppi, will also be taken into custody, and they'll all be charged with murder and racketeering. Juvieux plans to flip Battaglia and have him turn on the entire Chicago gangster scene, leading to the arrest of hundreds, maybe thousands, of criminals, breaking the empire for good. To him, he's personally removed, and this is going to be a big day.

Jones drives his car towards Reggi's home, parking it in a neighbor's driveway not far away where he can't be seen and he knows the residents are not home. He's done a few more lines before he left the house, so he is on edge and prepared to react, perhaps violently. In his back pocket is the arrest record of Reggi Paulson from decades ago, and he wants answers.

As he approaches Reggi's home on foot, he is understandably very angry after reading the work-up that Roger did on Reggi Thomas, and he's not satisfied even after having killed her son-in-law Edwin. When he comes within one hundred yards of the home, he sees Addie's car at the top of the drive in the small cul-de-sac. Before he can be seen, he steps behind a large tree, down the steep incline away from the road. Here he can still watch the house, and he begins to play the waiting game for Addie to leave.

After David, Addie, and Frank arrive at Reggi's home, parking at the top of the driveway, they have a short discussion before they leave the car.

Addie turns to Frank and tells him, "This is our operation, so let us do most of the talking. We're the law. You're here to give Reggi a friendly face to keep her calm. We know she's a senior citizen, and we are going to be very careful. I had a discussion with the departmental psychiatrist and we're pretty sure that Reggi has had a recurrence of her issue from years ago leading to all this lying about Ken Jones. Now we need to know what she knows. No more playing games. If at any point you think we are out of line, I want you to stop me and we'll have a side discussion. But this is our operation, and you need to let us do our job."

Frank simply looks at her and nods. He is solemn. He is serious. He's worried.

They walk down the driveway together and approach the door. Frank tries the doorknob and sees that it's unlocked. He sticks his head in and calls out to his mother. He hears her voice reply from deep inside the house, and he motions to Addie and David to remain put for the moment as he walks inside. Continuing to call out for his mother, he finds that she's in the laundry room, and he walks over and hugs her.

"Hi, Mom. Good to see you. What's new?"

"Frank, what a surprise. How nice of you to visit your old mom."

"Can I help you with the laundry?" he asks, reaching for wet towels.

She slaps his hand playfully, "Don't touch that, Frank. I know you're not here to help with laundry. It's going into the dryer anyway. What brings you out here?"

Frank looks at her seriously. "Adelaide is here, too, and she's with an FBI agent. They want to ask you some questions."

Reggi looks at Frank, and she asks, "Is this serious?"

"I think so, Mom."

As they walk towards the front door, they continue talking, and
Reggi asks, "What is this about?"

"I can't really tell you anything about this. They're going to be asking the questions, not me."

Reggi stares straight ahead, and when the door opens, she greets Addie warmly. "Hello, Adelaide. Are we looking forward to a wonderful wedding or what?"

Reggi looks behind Addie, and she finds a large man. He's wearing official FBI gear. After staring at him for a few moments, she extends her hand daintily and tells him, "I am Reggi Thomas. Why don't the three of you come in and I'll get us something to drink."

Juvieux takes her hand gingerly and tells her, "That would be great, thank you."

The three of them take a seat in the living room while Reggi ducks into the kitchen to get some iced tea. After she returns with a tray of refreshments, she takes a seat, and the four of them look at each other for a few moments.

This is going to be awkward, Frank is thinking.

Addie opens a folder and takes out a photograph. It's Helen's picture, and she shows it to Reggi. "Is this the person you saw that day in July at the top of the driveway of Ken Jones's home?"

Reggi glances at it. It's all she needs, and she exclaims happily, "Yes, that's her. How did you get it? How did you find her?"

Adelaide tells her, "She's been helping me with a case, and she's been looking at hundreds, maybe thousands, of photos to find *you*. Yesterday she saw your picture on my desk, the one from the Heritage Hills member files. Remember how we found you, that you were out walking your dog?" After seeing Reggi nod, she adds, "She recognized you."

Letting this sink in, Reggi replies, "I see, so now we know who the mystery woman is from that day."

Addie replies, "Yes, now we know who was in the area on that day." Addie is in inwardly thinking that if Helen didn't kill Elsie, and Gennarro Battaglia was away, the only other person in the immediate area was Reggi. Helen didn't see anyone else, and she found Elsie's freshly murdered body minutes later after having seen Reggi. But the idea is ridiculous that she would kill her, especially with something like a big, heavy bowl. Who does that? That's bizarre.

Addie delivers the shocker, "Also, yesterday while I was speaking with the person in this photograph, Ken Jones walked in."

Reggi's eyes begin to get a little larger and her lips are pursed.

"Ken Jones says that you're telling people that the two of you are marrying each other in a few months."

Reggi nods.

"Ken Jones says that you've told people that you bought a house together in Naples, Florida."

Reggi nods, "Yes."

"Ken Jones says you've told people that you take vacations together, sometimes weeks at a time."

And Reggi nods again.

"Ken Jones says that you've told people he's been to rehab and he completed it successfully."

Reggi continues to nod in agreement.

"Ken Jones says this is all lies."

Frank is looking to see his mother's reaction, which is one of skepticism and astonishment, and her defenses are going up.

Reggi quietly states, "Adelaide, why would you say something like this? Ken would never tell you these things. What are you trying to do?"

Addie replies, "Ken Jones is a retired mobster from Chicago. He moved here with his wife. She was murdered. And he told us the first time he met you was last week."

At this, Reggi stares back at Addie in disbelief, her mouth wide, her eyes wide defensively. She raises her voice and states the obvious, "You are calling me a liar." She raises her voice a little higher and states emphatically, "Adelaide, Ken Jones is lying. That's who the liar is!"

Addie calmly replies, "Someone is lying. That we know." She stares at Reggi and asks, "Can you tell us about your hospital stay from forty-three years ago?"

At this, Reggi stands up defiantly and almost screams, "I certainly will not. And I think you need to leave. If you think that I've been lying about my relationship with Ken Jones, then you are delusional!" Reggi dons her screwed up, angry face, contorted and ugly.

Reggi's voice begins to take itself to a higher and louder octave, "We're in love! We've been in a relationship for a long time! We're getting married to each other in Naples! He gave me a pony to use at his Wyoming ranch! I'm going to have access to all of his money! It's going to happen!"

She's out of control now, and Frank thinks she's going into the deep end again. "He bought this three-carat diamond ring for *me*! To show his love for *me*!" She takes it off and she gives it to Frank, "It's real! He loves *me*!" Pointing to her chest, glaring at Addie, she shouts, spitting it through clenched teeth, her face red, "*Me! Not you! Not anyone else! ME! ME! ME!*"

As Frank begins to look at the ring, it falls apart in his hands. The four of them are staring at it resting in pieces in his palm.

Frank sadly tells Reggi, looking into her eyes, hoping to calm her down, "Agent Juvieux here has been watching Jones's house for over a year and he's never seen you there."

"When Jones leaves the area, Agent Juvieux follows him, and he's never seen you with him. You don't have any pictures of the two of you together. All the stories about Ken and yourself are told to me by you. I never met this man until last week."

Before Frank can go on, she shouts at him, hissing, "We are in love! You're *stupid,* Francis!" She pauses a moment, then moves her twisted, ugly face closer to Frank and spits out, "*STUPID!*"

Frank looks at his mother and calmly says, "There's no romance with Jones, Mom. It's over."

Reggi stammers for a moment or two, then collapses onto her couch, sobbing. Between her heavy breaths and weeping, she tells the group, "The ring is fake. I made it up, this relationship with Ken Jones. It could be real. I just need more time. He and I could be in love." She sees the look on their faces, the look of pity. She looks down to her hands, "I just don't know anymore. What's happening to me?" She has the disposition of a frail old woman. It's all very depressing.

After she makes her confession, Frank thinks of all the quite real trips that she's taken with Ken Jones, his ranch, his home in Savannah, his rehab, his children, the yacht. It all seems so genuine, and he looks at his mother and asks, "This has been going on a long time. Did you write all this down to keep it straight?"

To which she replies, "I never wrote any of it down." Frank is miserable, his mother is mentally ill. You can't keep all those lies straight unless you experienced them yourself. Like reality.

Addie, David, and Frank stand up, and Addie articulates, slowly, "Reggi Thomas, you are a suspect in Ken Jones's wife's murder. You are not to leave the area. We are going to go to see Ken Jones now to inform him that you admitted the details of your relationship, and that you are now considered to be a suspect in his wife's death."

Addie then adds, looking at Frank, "You can't stay here with your mother. She's material to the case. You'll have to go with us."

The group of three depart leaving Reggi behind, seated on the couch.

Reggi doesn't even bother to stand up as they close the door behind them. After a while, she despondently rises and heads to her bedroom where the wall safe is waiting for her.

She opens the safe and takes out the Glock. She inspects the cartridge to make sure it's full. She then leaves her bedroom and walks to the bath off the living room. Once inside, she steps into the bathtub and closes the shower door. She doesn't want a mess, especially in her own bedroom.

Her thoughts turn to her husband Joseph and she quietly tells him that they will be together. She finds solace in that. She raises the gun to her temple. As she begins to pull the trigger, the doorbell rings.

She opens the shower door and looks out the window to see who her visitor is. She places the gun on the bathroom table, leaving the bath, and when she opens the front door she finds,

Ken Jones.

CHAPTER 23
DESTINY

May Day

> Destiny is for losers. It's just a stupid excuse
> to wait for things to happen instead of mak-
> ing them happen. Blair Waldorf

Battaglia sees Addie, Frank, and the FBI agent leave. As they pass by, he waits a few moments before he steps out from behind the tree. Crawling up the steep incline, he reaches the road and begins to walk purposely towards Reggi's home.

Overhead, he looks up after having felt a few drops of rain and sees the skies are black and heavy. At times they flash brightly from the lightning and almost immediate loud cracks of thunder. The weather mirrors his dark, cocaine-driven anger.

Approaching the front door, he rings the doorbell,

knocks on it, and, after a few moments, Reggi opens the door. "Hello, Ken," she remarks happily, "What a surprise to see you!"

Battaglia reaches out, smiles, replying warmly, "It's good to see you too, Reggi. Can I come in and talk with you a while?"

"Of course, please come on in. I have some iced tea out already. I just made it. We can share some refreshments and sit in the living room while we talk."

"Oh, that would be excellent. I hope you put some mint in it," and she nods as he follows her in.

Once they're seated, he assumes the role of Ken Jones and admonishes her, "Reggi I didn't see you at the club the other night for that fundraiser I told you about last week."

She replies, "Guilty as charged. I just couldn't make it. I had a lot of family events to plan for. Are you aware that my son is being married?"

He answers, "Yes. I am. I know the girl he's marrying. She's a detective."

"That's right. They haven't set a date yet, but there's just so much to do."

"Well, I can believe that." He's shaking noticeably from the cocaine.

"Is something wrong, Ken?"

"No, not at all. I was thinking about the car accident that your son was in. Addie was desperate to get to New York quickly, and I lent her my plane. I'm glad he's recovered." Then he adds, "I'm very wealthy, and I was happy to do it."

Reggi replies, "Well, we know a lot about each other. You *are* perceived to be the wealthiest member in the club."

He answers back, quickly, "And you are perceived to be the poorest."

She glares at him, "That's not a very nice thing to say."

"Well, I'm not a very nice man."

Taken aback, she asks, "What do you mean by that?"

He looks sideways at her and takes a sip of the iced tea that she poured for him, "You know I've heard a lot of stories recently."

Reggi, leading him, asks, "And?"

Ken continues, "I hear that you and I are quite the item."

She looks at him guiltily.

He rests his hand on her arm, "Someone told me that you and I are getting married." He chuckles a little, "Isn't that ridiculous?"

She laughs quietly along with him. "We just know each other. I don't know about getting married.

Who would say anything like that?"

Ken levels his gaze at her, "You would."

Appearing shocked, she answers, "What?"

She's a good actor, he thinks, "That's right, Reggi, you've been telling people that you and I take vacations together. That we buy property together. That your name is going to be on the deed. That I have a driver who takes us around because I get too drunk. That we're getting married soon. That's what you're telling people."

"No, I'm not."

"Yes, you are."

After a short pause while the two of them look at each other, he takes his hand off her arm. He then asks, "Do you know who I am?"

She replies shakily, "You're Ken Jones."

"Do you know what happened to my wife?"

"I heard that she passed away."

"Let me tell you who I am. My name is Gennarro Battaglia. I'm from Chicago. I ran a crime syndicate there. I'm a very bad guy. I'm connected. What I've done to my enemies would make your skin crawl. And I'll tell you this last piece of worthy information, and you can take this as solid advice, just for you. Someone killed my wife. And whoever that is, is going to die painfully. Tortured."

Reggi's eyes become very large and she looks confused and scared.

At that, Ken Jones pulls out the papers that he's been carrying in his pocket.

"What's that, Ken?"

"This is your arrest record from forty some odd years ago."

Reggi instantly becomes angry. She knows what's in it. "Where'd you get that? Give me that!" She hisses, reaching for the papers.

Holding the papers out of her reach, he says, "No way are you getting this. It says here that the reason you were arrested, and I quote, 'Subject attempted to inflict pain and injury to her husband through a repeated, blunt force impact to his facial cavity.' In other words, Reggi, you tried to smash his face in while he was sleeping. You tried to cave his face in with a heavy salad bowl. Just like Elsie, my wife, when I found her that day last July, the bloody bowl lying beside her."

A dark silence has entered the room. She can't meet his eyes.

Outside, the rain pelts the windows and fierce lightning and thunder can be heard.

Reggi replies quietly, "So what? So what if I killed her? She was in the way of us, of you and me." She looks at Ken Jones and begs him, "I know you feel the same way about me as I do for you. Oh Ken!"

WILLIAM CAIN

And she begins to cry.

Ken Jones looks at her with scorn and anger dancing wildly in his eyes, "You're pathetic. You killed the one person in the world I cared for deeply. My wife." He feels his uncontrollable anger welling up inside him. He's almost there, at his utmost anger, quickly formulating what his next moves will be to bring pain and death to Reggi, and closure for his wife.

After a long moment, Reggi excuses herself, "I have to go to the bathroom and get a tissue."

He watches her closely and tells her, "Keep the door open."

When she returns, Jones asks her, "Have you seen your son-in-law recently?"

"Edwin?"

Jones tells her, "He has some strange proclivities. Like little boys. I was with him earlier today."

She hisses menacingly, "What did you do to him?"

Ken answers, "Nothing, but if I did, I'd...well, let's not think about that. He wants my money. He thinks I'm marrying you. Look at yourself, Reggi. I can get any girl. My mistress is a stunning beauty. Not some old hag like yourself," he sneers. Then almost lightheartedly he changes the subject and continues, "Edwin and I entertained the company of two hookers this morning. Take a look at this picture." He shows her his phone message from the transvestite, Edwin bent over and the he-she behind him. "Really something, huh?"

She looks at his phone and she's disgusted with what she sees. Reggi begins to stand up and tells him, "I think you should leave now."

Ken Jones slaps her hard with his backhand, and Reggi cries out, but she doesn't defend herself. With his other hand, he grabs her throat and slams her backward, her head jerking. But she doesn't defend herself. He reaches into his pocket for the switchblade and pops it open, intending to inflict pain as he decides to remove her skin. But she still doesn't defend herself.

He lunges for her, pounces on top, and begins to strangle her with one hand, holding the blade close with the other, breathing heavily, smelly and hot. She doesn't move but instead looks straight ahead, staring impassively into his eyes. His grip is tightening, and she continues to simply lie there, looking at him. He suddenly thinks it's strange, this reaction of hers. She's not struggling.

And then he feels it. He loosens his grip and slowly backs away.

Ken quizzically asks her, staring at the gun she's holding, he's incredulous, "Where the hell did you get that from? Who keeps a gun in their bathroom?"

She levels the gun straight at his stomach, pulls

the trigger, and a crack louder than the lightning deafens the living room. A large hole appears in his back as the bullet makes its exit, and his tissue and blood are everywhere. No one is more surprised than Ken Jones. And no one hears. Most of the residents are still in Florida for their winter getaways. People are just now returning.

That's the beauty of Heritage Hills.

CHAPTER 24
THE END

May Day

New beginnings are often disguised as painful endings. Lao Tzu

F rank returns to his mother's home with Addie and David in tow. It's raining like hell, lightning is close overhead. Jones wasn't there when they knocked on his door. As Frank begins to walk down Reggi's driveway, a loud pistol shot rings out. It's definitely a blast from a gun, and he hurriedly starts to run towards the door. After the three of them enter, they briefly look around.

Addie's natural detective instinct now causes her to look over toward the freestanding coat rack. She sees an odd-looking coat. It's unusual. She walks over to the coat rack and pulls the coat away. It looks like a wrap with holes for arms with leather trimmed at the top and bottom. Looking in the lining of the coat she sees two letters: E.B. It dawns on her that this is Elsie's swing coat. Shit! It's been there for months, and she curses her own carelessness.

Ahead of her, Frank is calling out for his mother. As he walks into the living room, Reggi's back is to him and she's sitting, calmly staring through the sliding glass doors into the back of the house where the rain is falling heavily onto the deck. The lightning and thunder are closer now, and the black clouds are very low. At times, the room lights up as if from the flash of a camera, throwing dark, sinister shadows on the walls.

On the sofa, Reggi is thinking about her hus-band Joseph. She's thinking about Frédérica. She's thinking about Elsie. She's thinking about Ginger, her dog; her grandson Frannie comes to mind, all the money she lost, the cheap car she has to drive now, their hotel stay in Positano, Heritage Hills Country Club, Addie, weddings. She looks at her naked left hand. There's no ring there. She thinks about the cocktail parties, her daughter Megan, her daughter Charlotte, Edwin, Ken's vast wealth, jet setting.

She raises her heavy eyelids and focuses her eyes. Before her is Ken Jones, lying in a pool of blood, dying. "I'm so sorry for hurting you, but why did you attack me? The Ken Jones I know would never have done that. And we had such a bright future ahead of us." Her gun is leveled at Gennarro Battaglia.

With what little energy he has left, he rises to his knees, yelling to Addie, who has now also entered the room along with Juvieux, "She killed my Elsie!"

Reggi then calmly tells him, "I see you're in a lot of pain. Let's make it better." Before Addie can stop her, she holds the gun closer to Battaglia. Staring wildly at the huge barrel, he winces before she shoots him in the head, which jerks him backward violently and drives him onto the table behind.

David is just gaping in astonishment, his hands on his head. It's all happening so fast, out of control. There goes his state's witness, and his promotion, with her killing Gennarro Battaglia.

Then Reggi raises the gun to her temple. Addie quickly intervenes and yanks the pistol from her hand. She hears Frank crying behind her.

She turns to take him into her arms, and they embrace.

Addie finds she's crying, too.

Frank and Addie share one singular thought, that his mother is ill and needs help, and that they should have recognized it before all this killing. To end the madness. To prevent this pain and sadness.

They both turn their heads towards Reggi, who is looking through them with a blank, numb expression, devoid of comprehension.

Reggi begins to grin malevolently.

EPILOGUE

September

A symposium segment is given by Addie.

"This concludes my presentation of Maladaptive Daydreaming. To the subject, these daily, extended thoughts are real, detailed scripts played out for hours. Their experiences are as real as reality itself. One day, perhaps soon, this will become a more widely recognized mental illness. Thank you." Captain Henson walks off stage.

The bachelor dinner is underway for Frank's son, Frannie.

He looks over at his son and he knows Frannie's looking forward to his future with Agatha. In his toast to Frannie, he remembers the dearly departed. Reggi is one of them. He's had her declared passed away in order to protect his mother from the press.

A speedboat skims the waters, traveling quickly over Lake Lure, pulling a skier.

Gangi and Gen are in the boat with Jennifer, and behind them is Daphne on a single slalom ski. Gen's stomach wound has healed. The bullet didn't hit any organs. The headshot was off. Pistols are notorious for their poor aim. It struck him above the ear, near the rear of his head, biting off some skull, but his brain escaped impact. He's healed.

One hundred feet below the surface they're speeding over, Edwin is resting in his car until the end of time, in cold, dark, murky water, free from sunlight.

Gen tells Gangi that he'll be going away for a long time. Juvieux has arrested him for killing Riggoti. *Addie's not happy with him, but she'll get over it,* he thinks.

He looks over to Gangi and tells him, loudly above the din of the boat's engines, "I have an idea. It'll solve my problem *and* yours."

Weeks later, Helen calls from Australia using a video app.

Addie reaches to pick it up and Frank says, "You're answering a phone call from a former hitman living in Australia. Really? Captain?"

She replies, "Yes, Frank. Watch me."

When she picks up the phone call, she sees something is changed. Helen notices her surprised expression on the video call, "Don't look so shocked! I had a nose job, a little facelift. Best of all, I got new boobs. Hey, Addie, guess who's coming to see me?"

"Who?"

"You'd never guess in a million years. I'll give you a hint. He's bringing his daughter," she says happily.

When Addie ends the call and puts the phone down, she looks at Frank with a look of slight worry, "She's coming back to finish some business. I don't know exactly what that means."

Juvieux is disappointed. He arrested Battaglia, Gangi, and Michael.

But he's pissed. Battaglia won't turn state's evidence. Still, he has an idea. And that idea involves someone very close to Biggie Battaglia.

Two weeks later, during Frannie and Agatha's wedding reception, Frank is deep in thought, and he ducks into a small room where he can gather himself. He knows his mother needs help and her sickness has compelled him to reach out for what he wants and needs. Life's too short.

Addie joins him and he tells her, "I just need to get my arms wrapped around everything that's happened. It's not every day your mother is arrested for murder by your fiancé."

He looks at her and says, "Let's plan our wedding, beginning tomorrow. We deserve to be happy too. Let's plan our future."

Reggi's in a guarded mental facility on the outskirts of New York City, Woodside Psychiatric.

Reggi is seated outside on a bench staring into space, speaking to someone who's not there. She's more deeply in her fantasy than ever before, but she's happy. She believes Ken Jones is with her, and she talks to him animatedly.

She pauses, keeping her eyes beneath her hat, when a delivery truck arrives. It's the same truck every day, same driver. She's making a mental note on the time of day, the same as yesterday, and the day before that, and the day before that.

The truck parks in the same spot, around one hundred feet from where she's sitting. Just like it did yesterday. And the day before that.

And... just like the day before that.

To Be Continued
in

2020
With Book 3

and the ebook is free on five consecutive Mondays

Send an email to williamcainauthor@gmail.com,

get on the list,

and I'll tell you when

Thank you!

At this moment I'm thinking about my stories and my readers, and I want to write a thread that you'll like and believe in. I have ideas that I cook up and then throw away, and then there are some that are inspired by my readers. Use the email below and send me your thoughts, inspiration for my books is from you! Dedication for my books is FOR you!

I hope you enjoyed my writing as well as the storyline. If that's the case, won't you leave some feedback for me on Amazon. You may not know this, but I routinely give my eBooks away for free. If you 'like my page' on Facebook (william cain author), you'll receive notifications when I plan the next giveaway. As a rule of thumb, my ebooks are free on five Mondays every three months.

I'm planning eight more volumes with Addie. There's even a period piece based in Chicago that takes place in the forties, up to present day, and includes Addie meeting Biggie when she's just sixteen.

I'll continue to do my best, making the mystery harder to solve with each Volume as it's published, just like a crossword puzzle that's easy on Monday and almost impossible on Sunday. Humbly, thank you once again for reading my novel.

William Cain - williamcainauthor@gmail.com

Made in United States
North Haven, CT
11 December 2024

62245602R00162